The Flame

of

Telbyrin

A Tale of Heroism and Faith

Br. Benedict Dyar, O.S.B.

To: Bill

Thanks and many blessings!

— Br. Benedict

EMAIL QUESTIONS TO THE AUTHOR AT TO THE AUTHOR AT BRBENEDICTOSB@GMAIL.COM

© 2018 BY THE BENEDICTINE SOCIETY OF ALABAMA, DBA ST. BERNARD ABBEY

FIRST EDITION, 2018

ISBN 978-1-7907709-1-5

COVER ILLUSTRATION BY JODY POTTER

PUBLISHED BY EBOOKSTALKTOME, LLC

Dedication

To my parents, George and Peggy and Anna my sister; and to Abbot Cletus and my confreres at St. Bernard Abbey and to all of those who have walked with me on my journey of faith.

ᗑ ᗑ ᗑ ᗑ ᗑ ᗑ

"We are afflicted in every way, but not crushed; perplexed, but not driven to despair; persecuted, but not forsaken; struck down, but not destroyed."

2 Corinthians 4:8-9

Table of Contents

Prologue

T HE CREATOR SPOKE AND IT CAME TO BE. The Eternal Flame.
All peoples say that it was the center of the world. It was
the first spark of the world where the Creator's hand had
touched. It was not the Creator, but it was the visible symbol
of all creation's prayers that went up to the Creator. It was
the symbol of the Eternal Glory that all peoples gave to the
Creator; the Unnamable One.

All life clustered around it and spread out over the land.
As civilizations formed, there appeared the Vicars of the
Flame; the first of Elvenkind. Among them first was Cyrus,
Patriarch of all Elves, of the race that Fades. Cyrus and the
Vicars took a bit of the Flame to each civilization. To Humankind, they gave a bit of the Flame to Caltirion, the Great
City of Hallintor. Alrihon the First received it from the hand of
Cyrus. Cyrus then took it to the Wood Fays. There they hid
the Flame deep within the shades of the Great Forests. So
each people received with joy a bit of the Flame from Cyrus
and the Vicars, with which to give eternal praise to the Creator. Lastly, Cyrus took it to the Shadow People, the Meldron,
who lived deep within the Mountains of Black. They were the
only people who did not make the annual Pilgrimage to the
Flame, yet their desire was to be like the Creator. Ralharin,
their king, did not receive a bit of the Flame from the Vicars,
but scoffed saying:

"Elvenkind thinks they are the bringers of Divinity to
the whole world. Yet we know better. The Universe began in
Blackness, and in Blackness we will stay. We will be like the
Creator by discovering our own Flame. Leave us, Cyrus, and

come hither no more."

"Then your desire is not to give praise to the Creator?" asked Cyrus. Ralharin scoffed again.

"We will BE like the Creator. We will know the Eternal Secret, and from the Blackness we will discover it. You think that in this Flame you find Divinity, but you know not the Secrets of the Divine. Your flame is idolatry and a shame to the Creator. You know nothing."

"The Flame is not the Creator, Ralharin," said Cyrus. "Neither does it hold any secrets. It is a symbol of the eternal praise we give to the Creator. Join us. Won't you join the rest of Creation in the Eternal Song?"

Ralharin drew his sword.

"I told you to leave, Cyrus. Now you will pay the price for your obduracy. This is your final warning." Cyrus held up the bit of the Flame in his hand.

"No one can stop the Eternal Song, Ralharin. Not even you. The Flame represents it. All creation sings it. Let the Meldron give praise to the Creator."

Ralharin snarled.

"I will stop your song, Cyrus. And all the world will grieve over your death. We will see what becomes of the Song." Cyrus held up the Flame again.

Ralharin attacked.

The Flame then immersed Ralharin and burned him; his hands dropping the sword as he fought the burning blue Flame all around his body. He rushed into the darkness still trying to fight the Flame, crying out and holding his head as if he were hearing something that tortured him deep in his mind.

When it subsided, there emerged a voice from the rocks:

"An eternal antipathy between your race and mine, oh Cyrus. For you have caused this and hindered our quest. Your idolatrous Flame will be snuffed out and your Vicars put to route. Oh, Cyrus. I will never forgive nor forget!"

Cyrus faced the rocks.

"Your threats cannot stop the Song, Ralharin. A curse be upon your race. And cursed be your doctrine of blackness. All creation will sing to the Creator, Who is rightly to be praised, while you dwell in deathly silence, because you would not receive the gift of the Creator for this world nor the joy that goes with it."

Since that day Elf and Meldron have been mortal enemies.

From the Chronicles of the Vicars of Laerdiron.
Age Unknown.

Chapter 1

"GUARD! FORM RANKS!" SHOUTED ORILIN. THE SHOCK TROOPS snapped to battle formation; their circular shields covering one another. Spears overhung from the shields. The Meldron arrows rained down upon the shields.

"Steady!" shouted Orilin again. His troops slowly made way toward the Meldron infantry. The cavalry from Caltirion smashed into the enemy's right side which distracted the enemy archers.

"Break ranks!" Orilin yelled. "Attack!" The Guard hurled themselves into the fray. Orilin took up his spear and hurled it toward the center Meldron troop who was commanding the left flank, nailing him to the ground. He drew his sword and leaped upon them, hewing Meldron as he went. Caltirion's infantry took heart to see that the Guard had driven the Meldron ranks into a panic.

"Charge them!" yelled young Commander Lardin.

Orilin was trying to get to Karvol, slashing and hewing as he went. None were able to resist him. The dance of battle was upon him.

"Karvol! Come to me, you coward!"

Suddenly they were present; the Meldron sorcerers protected by their infantry. Many of the men of Caltirion panicked as the sorcerers hurled fire and lightning into their ranks. Many of them were slain.

"Elrad!" yelled Orilin. "Help those men!" The Vicar Elrad rode into the fray blocking the lightning with his staff; a bit of the Flame atop it. More fire and lighting were hurled. Elrad was not able to block all. More men were slain and Caltirion's forces wavered.

Orilin dove forward, grabbed a spear from the ground and hurled it, impaling one of the sorcerers with it. He then blocked fire with his shield, twisted and hewed another down with his sword. Suddenly a huge hammer smashed down upon Orilin's shield, breaking it. The Meldron lord Karvol attacked again. Orilin dodged and rolled across on his side. The hammer smashed down upon the ground, the shock felt by Orilin. Elrad dismounted and took to Orilin's side.

"Karvol!" he shouted. "You have lost!" The Meldron lord laughed.

"I never lose, Elrad!" He swung his hammer at the Vicar, but he dodged it. Karvol then kicked Elrad in the chest, sending him sailing. The Vicar smote his head upon a rock, knocking him unconscious. Orilin saw his chance. He attacked the Meldron, kicking him in the back of the knee and sending him down in pain. Facing him, Orilin smote the staff of the hammer with his sword, snapping the staff in two. He held up his sword.

"It's over, Karvol! Surrender!"

The Meldron laughed.

"It is over for you, Little Hawk." He drew a dagger and struck. It caught Orilin in the side.

"Agh!" he yelled. But he returned by smiting Karvol in the head cleaving his helmet and his skull. But there were still the sorcerers to take care of, and the Guard was barely holding them off.

ᐁ ᐁ ᐁ ᐁ ᐁ ᐁ

Orilin Alandiron shook himself out of his flashbacks and began playing his harp again, watching the sunset. His hands skillfully plucked the strings as he began to sing a song. The song was a deep semi-mournful, yet hopeful song. It was a song from Laerdiron; the giant ancient Elven city now destroyed by the Meldron. Orilin himself was an Elf. His race came in all shapes and sizes. Some were tall and strong, some were short and portly. Some Elves were fair-skinned, some were dark-skinned. Some even could grow facial hair. All, however, had ears that pointed to the sky.

Orilin himself was as tall as a Human. In the ancient tongue of Laerdiron, Orilin's name meant "Little Hawk." He was 301 years old. His parents had Faded after the destruction of Laerdiron and after they had given their infant child to the Vicars of Caltirion. Since the destruction of Laerdiron, the Elves had been a people living in exile among Humankind or in what were known as Enclaves. Kal-Ardaan and Barisath their king and queen had Faded.

One Elf, Elrad, was among the Vicars who took Orilin in. Elrad had raised the boy from an infant. Orilin grew into a strong Elf. He had blackish blue hair and ocean blue eyes. His pointed ears were sizable but not overgrown. Orilin was nimble yet strong and had shown promise in both swordsmanship and music. He learned to play the pipes and harp from Elrad. Martralin, an elderly Elf in the Lorinthian Guard, Caltirion's prized fighting force, taught him swordsmanship. Orilin developed into the best swordsman in all of Caltirion and also developed into a talented musician. He was joined to the ranks of the Lorinthian Guard when he was 205 years old.

Over the ages, the empire of Hallintor grew involved in more political squabbles and was slowly falling apart. Caltirion remained the bastion of the empire. People had grown lax in making the annual Pilgrimage to the Flame and there was war between various lords. Orilin fought defending Caltirion until he was 298 years old. After the Battle of Ash-Vargal in the Mountains of Black, with the defeat of the Meldron leader Karvol who led rebellious lords against Caltirion, Orilin was honorably discharged from the Lorinthian Guard. His armor he laid aside, but was allowed to keep his sword. So he picked up his harp, pipes and sword and sought for a life of quietness, tired and wearied from a life of violence. This happened during the early reign of King Lyrinias and the Arch-Vicarage of Hhrin-Calin.

When he was 300, he started to live on Alander Kesstal's cattle farm in West Sargna. Alander and his wife, Zitha, had one son, Drelas, and one daughter, Alanna. They had also employed a local Elven farm girl named Larilyn who had been raised in Acaida. She was close to Orilin's age and height, very comely and also played the pipes for the cattle. She had long black hair and grey eyes. Decorations of multi-colored yarn were in her hair. The two fell in love very soon. At the local city in Acaida, the marriage was blessed and she became his wife.

Orilin sat, continuing his song. The cattle were lowing in the background calling their calves. As he plucked the last notes on the harp, he heard footsteps behind him. Orilin smiled and turned around. It was Larilyn.

"Those footsteps could only be those of my beloved," he said.

Larilyn smiled.

"I put mineral in the bucket," she said.

Orilin looked over to her.

"Come and listen," he said. She smiled and nestled into him on the little knoll. Orilin played an Elven love song. It was one of Larylin's favorites. Orilin sang it with passion and Larylin smiled. As Orilin finished, he sighed and smiled, breathing in the fresh evening air. Larilyn put down his harp and embraced him.

"I love you," she said.

Orilin closed his eyes.

"I love you too." And he did so. Larilyn was almost like a dream. And he did not want to wake from it. She was the answer to his prayers after a long life of extreme violence that he never wanted to go back to. He wanted to stay here on this farm with her until the Fading. Everything about her was perfect. He touched one of her pointed ears, and she smiled.

"Ho, Orilin!' shouted someone coming down the road to the farm.

Larilyn laughed a little.

"That's Alander," she said. "He wants us to come to dinner tonight." Orilin looked toward him and chuckled a little too.

"Then we shall go. Zitha always has the best pies."

Larilyn nodded.

"She does."

The two picked up their belongings and started down the road where Alander was. Alander held his crook in one hand and a bucket in the other.

"Just finished putting up the chickens," he said. "It's a beautiful sunset. It should be a pretty night as well." Orilin looked up at the darkening sky and could see that the first star appeared.

"Ethlaharin," he said. "The star of Laerdiron."

Larilyn looked up.

"Some things can never be destroyed."

Alander looked up.

"It's Alanna's favorite star. You know she wants to be an Elf."

Orilin and Larilyn looked at each other and smiled.

"I suppose Zitha is cooking her pies tonight?" asked Orilin.

Alander looked back and smiled.

"Oh, yes. We have wanted you to come and eat with us for some time now. We have to get ready for the Pilgrimage."

Orilin nodded.

"Sargna's time is always the best. Caltirion always made theirs in summer. It was so hot."

Sargna always made their Pilgrimage at Al-Nartha, the Holy City, in the spring. Alander himself was a very devout man, but did not show his piety in a profound way. It was a life of simple faith. They started to walk back to the homestead.

"Drelas and Alanna want to meet with one of the Vicars," said Alander. "I wonder what could become of it."

Orilin looked up as he kicked a pebble with his boots.

"Elrad could be there," he said. "I'm sure he would give them his blessing."

"Oh, yes," said Alander. "Since he knows you, we could get them in to see him."

"Well, let's not jump to conclusions just yet," said Orilin. "It's still very hard to meet Elrad. But I do have my ways," he said cracking his knuckles.

Larilyn laughed a little.

"What ways are those?"

"Well, Elrad did teach me," said Orilin. "Hopefully he will give me the time of day."

Larilyn laughed again.

"Maybe you would like to introduce your wife to him

6

as well?" she asked.

Orilin looked at her and smiled.

"Yes. And to let everyone know that you are taken!"

She sniggered and took his arm.

The three reached the house at sundown. Alanna came running out to meet him. She was a girl of twelve and had long blonde hair. She came out with a set of pan pipes.

"Look, Orilin!" she said. "Look what I got from Trealin! He got them for me in Acaida. He doesn't know how to play them, but I told him that you would teach me." Orilin's eyes narrowed, and he smiled.

"It's a lot of hard work to get good," he said. "Are you ready?"

"Yes," she said. "I will play for people at the Pilgrimage!"

Orilin nodded.

"Okay. I'll teach you."

"Yes!" she said and ran off to the house.

"Trealin dotes on her," said Alander. "She will try to learn anything these days."

Orilin smiled as he cleaned off his boots at the entrance to the house.

"It's good to learn new things. She will have a great time learning it during the Pilgrimage."

Alander nodded.

"All right. Time to eat."

When they entered the house, Zitha had everything ready. She was busying around the dining room still in her grease-smeared apron. Her brown hair was tied back and she placed fresh pies out on the table.

"We are so glad you came, you two," she said. "How was the herd today?"

"Great," Orilin replied.

Zitha sat down the rest of the dinner.

"Were there any calves born today?"

Orilin shook his head.

"Not since that one two days ago."

The rest of the family sat down to get ready to eat. Young Drelas, a boy of eight, looked up at the Elves.

"Do you think I will get to meet Elrad?"

Orilin smiled and looked at him.

"You should be able to if he is there. I'll see what I can do. The Wood Fays will be there also."

The two children looked at each other. Alanna smiled and applauded.

"Yes! I've always wanted to see the Wood Fays. Do you think they will listen to me play?"

Zitha laughed a little.

"How about we pray first," she said.

Alander led them in a prayer to the Creator, and the dinner commenced. Truth be told, Zitha was a little scared of the stories of the Fays. Some people who ventured in their forests did not come out for quite some time.

"Zitha, they are nothing to worry about," said Orilin. "Zarkaia will certainly dote on Alanna."

"Is she their queen?" asked Alanna.

"Oh, yes," Orilin said. "And she loves children."

That comment made Zitha even more worried. She trusted Elves, but she had never met the sprites of the Great Forests.

"Oh, I want to be an Elf," said Alanna. "I would be even better at playing the pipes than you, Orilin. Because I would have the years of practice!"

"Perhaps," said Orilin.

Larilyn laughed a bit, putting down her mug. Alander spoke up then.

"In two days we will leave for our Pilgrimage to the Holy City. That should give you two enough time to get ready, shouldn't it?"

Orilin and Larilyn nodded.

"Who will care for the cattle while we are away?" asked Larilyn.

"Trealin said he and his family would look after them. Then they would go on Pilgrimage after us."

"All right," replied Orilin.

"Orilin, I'll need your help with security," said Alander.

"Yes," said Zitha. "There have been robbers reported on those roads."

Orilin nodded gravely. He did not relish the idea of unsheathing his sword. Larilyn could tell he was in deep thought.

"While Orilin guards us," she said to Alanna, "I can help you with your pipes!" Alanna smiled at this.

"Thank you, Larilyn!" The Elf touched a lock of her long, blonde tresses.

"I think we can put some Laerdiron yarn in this hair."

Alanna beamed.

"Did you here that, mother? I'm going to look like an Elf after all!"

Chapter 2

T WO DAYS PASSED. THEY WERE SEMI-CLOUDY DAYS WITH no rain. Orilin and Larilyn did some finishing touches with the herd in preparation for Trealin and his family.

"I think they will miss your pipes, love," said Larilyn. Orilin grinned.

"Perhaps Trealin will play for them."

"Ha!" laughed Larilyn. "I'd like to see him try!"

"They would probably stampede him," said Orilin. Larilyn grinned.

"I'll stampede you!" She threw some fresh hay in his face.

Orilin grinned, laughed and closed his eyes. He then brushed the hay out of his face and hair and looked at his wife.

"You asked for it!"

The two got into a hay fight in a fresh pile. Alander was making his way over to the barn and could hear the laughing and squealing. Orilin and Larilyn rolled in the hay. They laughed uncontrollably and continued to throw the hay at each other. It was then that Alander rounded the corner.

"What are you two doing?" he asked. Orilin and Larilyn looked up from the hay pile; the dust and hay all over their heads and bodies. There was a moment of awkwardness, and then the two started laughing, getting up and brushing off.

Alander shook his head.

"Elves," he said. He walked back and began getting the wagon ready as the two Elves continued laughing.

ᘯᘯᘯᘯᘯᘯ

The Kesstals and their Elven friends started their long journey to Al-Nartha, the great city where the Eternal Flame was housed in a great temple. It was going to be a long journey. There were the robbers to worry about, of which Orilin was not too concerned. There was the Forest of Beth. No Wood Fays lived in the forest that anyone knew about. It was a rather piney forest where a few woodcutter settlements and homesteads were. Then it was a journey across the plains to the river, and the family would take a ferry to Al-Nartha.

The packhorses carried Alander's wagon. Zitha and the children were in the wagon with the supplies and necessities. Orilin and Larilyn each rode on a horse next to Alander. The two Elves were playing a melody on their pipes. It was a duet of sorts. Orilin would play one part on his pipe and Larilyn would respond with her part. Then the two would join in for measures at the same time. This duet continued for a very long time. Orilin and Larilyn would sway a little to the music. Alanna was loving it. Even though the duet was going on forever, she was trying to pick up the melody on her own pipes.

"All right. That's enough of that!" said Alander finally. "Play something different."

The two Elves laughed. Alanna chuckled a little as well. Drelas rolled his eyes.

"Don't ask to learn how to play that one," he said. "They will never stop playing it."

"I kind of liked it," she said. "Hey Orilin. What kind of melody was that?"

Orilin looked over to her.

"It's a travel melody. It's one of Larilyn and my favorites."

"I can tell," muttered Alander.

"Can I learn how to play it?," she asked.

"Sometime," sniggered Orilin.

The Elves and the Kesstal's were making their way into the Forest of Beth the next day. Many songbirds and squirrels greeted them on their way. Larilyn would hold out assortments of nuts for the squirrels and they would light on her hands and chew them. Orilin would smile.

"Cute little squirrel," she would say. And she would let it go.

"Where we come from we eat them," said Drelas. Zitha slapped him a little on the shoulder and put a finger to her lips. Larilyn turned to him with a grin.

"Maybe there are some big ones here in this forest that would eat little boys."

Drelas rolled his eyes and sighed.

"Why is everything so funny to Elves?" he asked.

Larilyn laughed. Drelas shook his head.

"You see," he said.

Zitha looked at him.

"You could do with some cheering up yourself, young man. It's not that much longer until we stop for the night."

"This trip is taking forever."

"We are only two days into it," said Zitha, "And now you are already starting to complain?"

Drelas sighed and crossed his arms.

"Don't worry, Drelas," said Alander. "We will be in Acaida tonight." Drelas nodded. He knew he was being a bit petulant, but he really did not understand Elves. His parents thought he was being childish but, in his opinion, Elves were one of the most childish races in Telbyrin. Yet he knew somehow the world would not be the same without them.

"Hey Larilyn," he said. The Elf woman turned to him.

"Yes, love," she smiled.

"Sing a song about Laerdiron."

Larilyn's countenance went somewhat thoughtful and serious. She then closed her eyes and smiled. The song that came forth was beautiful and went on for some time. Larilyn sang of the joys of the great Elven city. Nothing was sung of its downfall except a hint of it being reestablished one day. Orilin listened, smiling as some tears welled up in his eyes. Larilyn finished the song and took a deep breath.

Drelas sat stunned a little. The family rode on in silence.

After some time Drelas spoke up.

"Did you ever see the city?" he asked.

Larilyn smiled at him a little.

"No, dear. I was born around the time of its destruction; about the same time as Orilin. We both just missed it. But my parents knew it. Oh … they did." Drelas was curious. Alanna sat with eyes cast down a little. She wanted Laerdiron to come back.

"What … happened to your parents?"

Larilyn's mouth opened a little and she hesitated. Orilin turned around instantly, held up his hand slightly and shook his head "No." Drelas nodded a little and looked down.

They made their way into a brief clearing out of the

forests. It was getting towards evening as they traveled along. They passed by a farm. There was a woman beating out laundry and scrubbing it. There was a man splitting firewood; some dogs barking at them. There were two kids playing with balls looking at them curiously. The field they journeyed through next was filled with blooming wildflowers. Orilin sat up in his saddle.

"We should not be that much farther. I can see the smoke rising in the distance."

"I hope so," said Zitha. "I'm getting kind of worried. It's getting dark."

"Don't worry," said Orilin. They went through another section of the Forest. Alander and Orilin spurred on the horses at a quick trot. Zitha was getting very nervous. Robbers could be waiting around the corner. They went over a hill of various pines and down a ravine. A small river was flowing past them and a covered bridge lay in front of them. It was the bridge leading to Acaida.

"Finally," said Zitha. "Let's hurry." The family made their way across the covered bridge and then they could see the lights of Acaida and the smell of wood burning. They rode further and could then see the gates. Two guards stood posted outside with torches beside them.

"Who is it?" one asked.

Orilin sat up.

"Orilin and Larilyn Alandiron and the Kesstal family."

The guard sniggered.

"It's those Elves," he said to the other. "You know the two that play those pipes?"

The other grinned.

"Come on in," he said. "Weapons inspection first." They looked at Orilin's sword.

"This is the only weapon you have?" Orilin nodded.

"A sword from Hallintor," said the other.

"Come on," said Orilin. "I'm not going to hurt you." The two looked at each other and laughed.

"We remember you from last year," they said. "You and your pretty wife there. Master Elimed will be looking for you. Come on in."

The party rode past the guards. Larilyn looked to her husband.

"Elimed will be glad to see us, love. Maybe we could stay with him?"

Orilin nodded.

"That is a thought. It would save on gold."

"Excellent idea," said Alander.

Acaida was very crowded, and the party assumed that most of the inns would be filled up with travelling pilgrims.

"We got here too late, Alander," said Zitha. "We will never get a room. And who knows if the Vicar will let us stay with him."

"Don't chide, dear," said Alander. "If need be we can stay in the wagon. But Orilin here will see to it that we get somewhere suitable."

Orilin looked at him and shrugged.

"I can't fix everything, but Elimed should take us in for the night."

The party rode down the road further until they passed a tavern.

"Ah," said Alander. "I've been waiting for…"

"No," said Zitha. "Lodgings first."

Larilyn looked to Orilin.

"You think we will have to ride all the way to the shrine?" she asked.

"I hope not. But then…"

"Ho, Orilin! Uh … Arban, that animal's …" It was Elimed, the town Vicar. He was coming out of a man's home.

"I told you I'm closed, Elimed," said the man. "We will get that horse of yours shod in the morning. You're starving my poor children."

Elimed shook his head.

"Anything you say, Arban."

Orilin looked and saw that the farrier Arban's house was closed. Elimed could be somewhat of a pest. He started toward Orilin.

"Such an irreverent man," said Elimed. "Won't even give his Vicar a little help in a pinch."

"Nah," Orilin replied. "He's just hungry." The three Elves laughed.

Elimed had a short-kempt grey beard and grey hair. It was at various ages that Elven males could even think about growing facial hair. Orilin had not sprouted one.

"Elimed, it's getting crowded," said Orilin. "Do you know ..."

"The vicarage, of course," he said. "I insist. I've been so wanting to see you two again. Good food, good drink. You can't beat it. I have a good barrel of ale that I have not yet opened. Better than that swill they serve in that place," he said pointing to the tavern. "Come on."

Orilin grinned.

"You see how easy that was?" he said to Alander.

"Hmm," he replied. "You said you couldn't fix every-thing."

The families rode down the road with Elimed politely pushing people out of the way. It was pitch-black night now. An array of stars could be seen overhead.

"Just a little farther," said Elimed. "The night is busy with the pilgrims. Tomorrow's going to be even busier with people getting their supplies and all. I'll be traveling one day behind you. Got some things I need to finish up with here first."

"What things?" asked Orilin.

"Well, there is this darn horse. I was going to get Arban to come look at her tonight since I'm in such a hurry. I wanted to get her foot looked at before this house blessing I have to do tomorrow. There is nothing exciting in this town. It seems all I do is house blessings and weddings."

Larilyn looked at him.

"Hey! What about our wedding?"

Elimed looked back.

"Well … naturally yours was the best. I have not seen a better couple in all of Acaida. It is a love worthy of a saga like …"

"Elimed, please," said Orilin. "What's for dinner?"

"Aghhm," he coughed. "Only the finest at the vicar-age. You know how people dote on me, Orilin. 'Master Elimed, please take this pie from us. Master Elimed, please take this roast pheasant from us.' Every week it is like that. It's a wonder I'm not rolling down the street."

They arrived at the vicarage. It was a simple one-story house with a red-tiled roof. Elimed tied up the horses for them and watered them. His horse did not like the strange horses being next to her. She neighed a bit, but Elimed had a strange way of calming her down. The horses were then fed and the wagon was parked. Alander and Zitha thanked Elimed for the room in his vicarage. Even though the house was one story, there were three bedrooms. Small though they were, they were very nice. Towards the back of the vicarage was a garden. It was very large; a place for many visitors. Elimed tended it himself. There was a cobblestone walkway that ran through the middle of the lawn and led to the Sanctuary. The family moved their belongings in the vicarage and looked around a bit.

"Make yourselves at home," said Elimed. "I'll tend to dinner."

"I'll help," said Zitha.

"Oh, no," said Elimed. "You are my guests. Relax. I insist." Dainties and cordials were brought out to them of various sorts. Drelas and Alanna were very impressed with the vicarage. They looked around with the light that the candles provided. There were statues and paintings on the walls. Most of them were Elven, but some of them were Hallintorian. Drelas looked out one of the windows towards the garden. Larilyn stood behind him.

"There's the Sanctuary," he said, "Where the Flame is housed."

Larilyn smiled.

"Yes. It is indeed."

Drelas looked back at her.

"That's where you and Orilin were married."

Larilyn nodded.

"Does every couple have to be married in front of a bit of the Flame?"

"No," said Larilyn. "But it is ideal. Orilin and I were fortunate to have it so. All that's required for a marriage is a Vicar present."

"Is Elimed the only Vicar in Sargna?"

Larilyn laughed a bit.

"Of course not. Vicars have to travel around a lot. But most of the ones in Sargna stop by monthly to see the Flame here in Acaida. Elimed is the oldest Vicar in Sargna and was a Vicar of Laerdiron."

"Really?" said Drelas. "Then that means he is pretty old!"

"1513 years!" said Larilyn.

"Just you wait, young one," said Elimed from the back. "Some day you will get old."

Drelas looked at Larilyn and smiled.

"Can we see the Flame after dinner?" asked the

boy.

"Yes," said Larilyn. "Orilin and I can take you there. Although you will see the main Flame in a few days."

"I still like it," he said.

Larilyn nodded.

The family sat down to a great dinner. There was the roast pheasant that Elimed had described and the pies. There was a peculiar Elven bread and salad full of nuts and raisins with an even more peculiar dressing. Alanna was eating mainly that in order to appear more Elven. Then there was the wonderful ale which Elimed bragged on. Everyone was surprised at how much Elimed enjoyed it.

"How many people do you think will be at the Flame in a couple of days?" asked Alander.

"It's going to be crowded with the Fays there," said Elimed. "But you should not have too much trouble. The Fays like to be by themselves."

"Don't they love children?" asked Alanna.

"Yes," said Elimed. "You will have to visit their Great Forests sometime."

Zitha did not look enthused.

The dinner went on with much conversation about the Pilgrimage and about Elimed's current duties in Acaida. The meal was finished up with a creamy pudding. Alander and Zitha looked as if they were getting sleepy.

"Well. Looks as if some of you are nodding off," said Elimed. "Shall we close with a blessing?"

"Yes," said Drelas. "Then can we see the Flame … if it is not too much trouble?"

"Why yes," said the Vicar. "We most certainly can. Perhaps Orilin and Larilyn would like to come along?"

Orilin and Larilyn nodded.

"Well, I'll be at the main one in a few days," said

Alander. "Thank you, Elimed. I think the wife and I will retire."

"Agreed," said Zitha. "Thank you, Elimed."

"My pleasure," said the Vicar. He led the families in a closing blessing. Everyone then helped put things away.

Chapter 3

THE NIGHT WAS GETTING A BIT COOLER. THE stars shown bright, and the star of Laerdiron shown brightest atop the zenith. Orilin and Larilyn led the children to the entrance of the Sanctuary. Elimed followed behind with the keys and a small lit taper. He passed them and took out a large silver key with a peculiar rune on it.

"Stay quiet in here," he said. "We are in the presence of the first spark of the world." The children nodded. Orilin looked up. A shooting star shimmered over the Sanctuary. A groan accompanied the iron door opening, and Elimed stepped inside leading the way. He then lit a few candles and the group stepped inside. Along the wall were engravings of the various races: Elves, Humans and Wood Fays receiving the Flame. Then in the front was a statue of the Patriarch Cyrus holding the Flame.

Then they saw it. Under the statue, in an intricate alcove was the bit of the Flame. It was a cool blue and it burned with joy. It gave off no scent but illumined all around it in a wonderful blue light. Orilin and Larilyn smiled. The children looked in wonder.

"Wow," said Drelas. "I love it every time I see it."

"I've forgotten how beautiful it is," said Alanna.

"Nothing feeds it," said Elimed. "It just burns. It is a wonderful gift of the Creator to us. Shall we pray?"

"Yes," they said.

Elimed led them in a very solemn prayer. In the prayer was the story of the creation of Telbyrin and the praise that the races gave to the Creator. Then there were words of thanksgiving of all that the Creator provides. Elimed ended the prayer with further words of praise to the Creator. The group sat in silence for a while. There were some pews in the nave of the Sanctuary and the children sat down. Orilin and Larilyn walked around the perimeter looking at the various works of art that so elaborately decorated it.

"I need to go to bed," said Elimed. "You are welcome to stay as long as you like. The door locks behind you."

"Thank you, Elimed," said Larilyn. The children responded likewise. Drelas and Alanna stayed there for a while longer until they were yawning.

"We have a long day tomorrow," said Larilyn to Alanna. "Shall we be putting you to bed?"

"Sure," she said. "I am getting tired."

"Let's get you to bed then," said Larilyn. "Come along, Drelas." The boy nodded and followed the Elf woman out of the Sanctuary. Orilin was still in prayer about something but looked up to his wife.

"I'll be here a while longer," he said.

"Don't worry," she said. "I'll be back."

"I'll leave the door propped open," he said.

Larilyn put the kids to bed. As she was tucking in Alanna, she looked up at Larilyn with sleepy eyes.

"Larilyn."

"Yes, dear?"

"Do you think Laerdiron will ever come back?"

Larilyn smiled but then sighed.

"What do you think?"

Alanna closed her eyes.

"I would like to think so. When I grow up, I want to live among the Elves; with you and Orilin … in Laerdiron."

Larilyn smiled again.

"Perhaps there will be that day. Do you believe it?"

Alanna nodded a bit.

"Then perhaps it will happen. Ethlaharin will always watch over you. Go to sleep, now." Larilyn sang the girl an Elven lullaby and the girl was fast asleep.

She gently closed the door and went back out into the night toward the Sanctuary. She walked in through the open door to where Orilin was. She took his hand and the two walked toward the Flame and sat down on one of the pews.

"Are they asleep?" asked Orilin.

"Yes," said Larilyn. "I'm not too far behind them."

Orilin smiled and embraced her a bit.

"Getting tired?" She nodded and laid her head on his shoulder.

"Remember our day?" she whispered.

"How could I forget?"

"Not just that day. The other one too."

"When I saw you?"

"Yes. I knew I had found you."

Orilin hugged her tightly.

"I knew I had found you too."

There was a brief silence.

"Orilin ... I'm sorry. I'm ... trying ..."

"Larilyn," he whispered. A tear ran down her cheek.

"Is that what you were praying about?," she asked.

Orilin looked down at her.

"Yes. But I'm also praying more so that you won't be upset. I don't want you to despair. You will always be my soul-mate. Always. That will never change. Like I said, I knew that I had found you. As surely as Ethlaharin shines, you are my soul-mate. Forever."

Larilyn started to weep a little and Orilin hugged her.

"My love," he whispered. "My love." They sat there for a long time, Larilyn clinging to his arm weeping. Tears started to fall from his eyes as he sighed. She had suffered enough. "O Creator," he prayed. "Don't let her suffer more."

$\Upsilon \, \Upsilon \, \Upsilon \, \Upsilon \, \Upsilon \, \Upsilon$

They stayed in front of the Flame for a long while. Larilyn eventually fell asleep and Orilin placed her head down on a pillow that lay in the pew. He was going to have to carry her out. She was so tired. He took her in his arms. She groaned a little and placed her arms around his neck. When she grieved, she always felt tired. And so he carried her out singing softly to her.

He blew the tapers out and went towards the door. Suddenly the whole room went dark. A cold chill ran through the Sanctuary like a wind on a winter day. The bluish glow ceased. Orilin turned around and was horrified at what he saw. The bit of the Flame was out.

"O … Creator!" he gasped. "O Creator!"

Larilyn awoke.

"What is it, love?" she asked groggily.

"Look!" he said.

Larilyn looked toward the Sanctuary alcove.

"Oh!" she cried.

Orilin put her down.

"Ahhh!" she cried. "My Creator!"

Orilin panicked. He did not want to leave her.

"I … I'll get Elimed," he said.

"I'm … I'm going …"

"Let's go!" he cried. The two Elves ran outside. Orilin burst into the house and ran into Elimed's chambers. Elimed was sound asleep until Orilin rushed over to his bedside.

"Wake up, Elimed!" whispered Orilin vigorously. "Wake up."

"Wha … what is this?" he groaned.

"Elimed," said Orilin. "The Flame is out. The Flame is out!"

Elimed awoke.

"Out!?" he scoffed. "What do you mean out? The Flame has burned since Telbyrin was created …"

"Elimed!"

Orilin practically pulled him out of bed.

"Come on!"

Elimed pulled on his robe and sandals and followed Orilin outside. Larilyn was waiting outside practically hysterical. The three ran into the Sanctuary and there stood the alcove … the Flame out.

Elimed questioned them.

"How long were you in here?!" he growled. "What did you do in here?!"

"There was nothing done, Elimed!" said Orilin firmly. "We were just praying."

"Praying?! Is that all?!" Larilyn looked to her husband and panicked.

Orilin stepped in front of his wife.

"We didn't do anything," he said. "She fell asleep, I picked her up and carried her out and it went out."

Elimed fumed at them for a bit, but slowly regained his composure.

"When did it go out?" he asked finally.

"I told you," Orilin replied. "When I was carrying my wife out."

Elimed breathed hard and narrowed his brows. There was a long silence.

"You two could not have put the Flame out," he said lowly. "I should have known that. I'm sorry that I …"

"It's okay, Elimed. Now what's going on?!"

"I don't know, boy," he said. "I don't know. Just … let me think." There was a nervous silence. Only the crickets could be heard outside. Elimed continued to breathe deeply.

"There are many things that might have happened," he said. "'Might' being the key word."

"So?" said Orilin.

"I don't know!" huffed Elimed. "Perhaps there is Meldron sorcery. Perhaps a very grievous sin. Perhaps …"

"So what do we need to do!?"

"There isn't much you can do right now, boy. Protect your wife … protect your loved ones. I suspect there is something dire going on in the world. And that's an understatement!"

"Shall we wake up the Kesstals?" asked Larilyn.

"No," said Elimed. "Let them stay as they are. I … I need to ride to Caltirion. I will search out Hhrin-Calin; he is in Caltirion this month. We desperately need to speak with him. He will know what to do."

"When are you going?" asked Orilin.

"Tonight!" replied the Vicar. "This is one of the largest … if not the largest catastrophe the world will see. If the Flame is out … then the question must be whether the Creator's care and protection still abides with us. The Flame was the symbol of that. And now that it is out …"

There was an awkward silence.

"Yes?" asked Orilin.

Elimed sighed.

"I don't know."

"Well," said Orilin. "What about your horse? She needs the farrier."

"We will have to try to shoe her ourselves. We have to leave tonight."

"What do you mean 'we?'"

"You're coming with me," said Elimed. "I can't do this without you, Orilin. I need the protection of the greatest swordsman of Caltirion. Who knows what malice is lurking in the world now? And the Vicars might indeed be the target! Besides, King Lyrinias is your dear friend. He can give us counsel along with Hhrin-Calin. If the Meldron are planning something, I'll need you."

"Whoa!" said Orilin. "I can't just up and leave. I have a wife and the Kesstals to look after …"

Elimed grabbed him by the shoulders.

"Orilin, this is the largest emergency ever! You may be facing the largest trial you have ever faced."

"I've left that life!" said Orilin. "I don't kill anymore, nor do I …"

"I don't care!" yelled Elimed. "You are an Elven warrior and will always be one! When the world needs your help and calls on you, you reply!"

"I can't," said Orilin.

"Yes you can!" replied Elimed. "Orilin, it's not just the world that is in danger, but possibly your wife and loved ones as well. You will be protecting them! If the Meldron …"

"You keep saying the Meldron. How do you know it's them?"

"I don't," replied Elimed. "But it seems like a logical guess to me. You ride with me tonight!"

There was another silence. Larilyn clung to her husband's arm.

"Not without her," said Orilin.

Elimed shook his head.

"This quest is not meant for her. It could be too dangerous."

"No," said Orilin. "I will not just leave my wife here in Sargna while who knows what runs around the world. If there is this danger you speak of, then I will see her safely behind the walls of Caltirion."

"Larilyn does not have skills in war," said Elimed. "She does …"

"You assume too much, Elimed. We don't even know if there is a war. But if there is danger, I will see her safe! Otherwise, I will not go with you."

There was another silence. Elimed slowly nodded.

"Hah," he sighed. "Have it your way, Orilin."

"On this matter, absolutely," he said.

Elimed shook his head again.

"We pack light. Tonight is going to be a long ride. And I do not want to alert the whole town just yet."

"The town will panic if you leave them, Elimed," said Larilyn. Let Orilin and I ride to Caltirion. You need to stay to console the people."

Elimed stared at them harshly.

"I need to talk to Hhrin-Calin," he said.

"You need to console the people," said Orilin. "Larilyn has a good point. The people need their Vicar. There could be riots and panicking all over Acaida."

Elimed pondered over their words.

"I see your point," he said finally. "Fine. Take the road north through the Dreath Wood. Don't go around it. The wood will conceal you. If the Meldron or other untoward peoples are about, it is your best bet."

"That wood is haunted," said Orilin. "The spirit of Kharlia haunts it, plus the ghouls. That place has been accursed ever since the Battle of Janlar."

"No need for a history lesson, Orilin," said Elimed. "Just go through the wood. Not at night preferably. Just go through it. You know how to get to Caltirion from the wood."

"We'll take the ferry across into Gallinthrar," said Orilin. "We'll ride hard from there."

"Good," said Elimed. "I'll take care of the Kesstals and explain to them everything."

Orilin nodded.

"I'll find Elrad as well as Lyrinias," he said. "Elrad has always counseled me in the right way."

Elimed smiled and nodded.

Elimed then guided them out from the Sanctuary back into the vicarage. He went to the supply closet and pulled out an old rucksack that went across the shoulder.

"I've had this thing for a long time," he said. "Now it's yours. I'll put some supplies in for you and a few survival tools. Here is some gold for you. You'll need it."

Elimed pulled out the gold pieces from a drawer and put them in Orilin's hand. Then he opened the cupboard and started to pack supplies in the rucksack with haste. There were two loaves of bread, a small wheel of cheese, some nuts and dried fruit. He opened back up the dusty closet and pulled out a water skin.

"I almost forgot this," he said. "Get some water from the fountain outside. The rivers and streams, as you know, will be fine for drinking water as well."

"I can carry these, love," said Larilyn to her husband. She took from him the rucksack and the water skin. Orilin nodded. He then crept back silently into the bedroom to pick up his and Larilyn's instruments and his sword. He slung the baldric around his shoulders, picked up the other items and left the room quietly. Then he rejoined Larilyn.

"Hhh," sighed Elimed. "Let me give you a blessing."
The two bowed their heads. Elimed blessed them and put his
hands on their shoulders.

"Go with all speed," he said. "And may we see happier days."

Chapter 4

THE TWO ELVES RODE INTO THE NIGHT, OR what was left of it. They had left a short note for the Kesstals explaining why they were taking their horses. Larilyn had written a special note for Alanna:

"Dear Alanna. My little Elven sister. I have gone on an adventure of greatest importance but I will come back to you. We will get those yarns in your beautiful hair after all. Be brave, listen to Elimed and wait on me. I will come back to you. Your big sister, Larilyn"

Orilin, in a note to Alander and Zitha, had advised them to go back to the farm. But he knew that was going to have to be their choice. They rode across the plains as the stars shown bright overhead. Hilmod, the star of Caltirion, shown in the north.

"Oh, Creator," prayed Orilin. "Do not forsake us." They continued to ride until they knew the horses were getting exhausted. They stopped by a little stream, clear as crystal, and watered the horses. They jumped out of the saddles onto the ground and sat down by the stream. Larilyn drank from the water skin and then handed it to her husband.

"Drink, dear," she said.

Orilin took the skin from his wife and drank a long draught.

"We should stop here for now, love," he said. "I don't think the horses can take any more. And we haven't slept since yesterday morning."

Larilyn nodded.

"I agree. Do you think I need to watch though?"

"I think we will be okay without a watch here," said Orilin.

"Okay," replied Larilyn. "Sleep, love." The two fell asleep nestled under an old blanket they got from the Kesstal's wagon. The night was still cool.

ᐱ ᐱ ᐱ ᐱ ᐱ ᐱ

Larilyn slept deeply. In it she saw stars and a beau-tiful city that she could only perceive to be Laerdiron. In it were beautiful gardens and trees. Pipes and harps could be heard from balconies. There was a beautiful Elven couple standing in a courtyard beside the Sanctuary holding a little baby Elven girl. They sang to the baby, and the mother held her to her breast.

Larilyn saw inside the Sanctuary. It was beautifully decorated. The Flame glowed. The mother continued to sing to her baby from the outside. Suddenly there was a shadow that filled the Sanctuary. There was a dark figure in the corner and then the Flame went out. The mother looked up from her nursing.

"Stay back," she hissed. The figure from the corner crept closer. All turned darker. Larilyn then woke up.

Orilin felt her jerk and throw off the blanket. She awoke breathing hard and holding her head with one hand. Orilin caressed one of her ears.

"What is it, love?"

Larilyn took his hand.

"I saw them, Orilin," she said. "I saw them."

"Saw who?"

"My parents, I imagine." she said. "There was a darkness, a blackness in the corner like a shape; a shape of a person. Then the bit of the Flame went out in the Sanctuary."

Orilin got up and sat beside her.

"It was a bad dream," he said. "Go back to sleep."

Larilyn shook her head.

"I can't," she said. "Besides, it's almost morning. We need to get started. Look there in the east."

Orilin turned and saw the first signs of dawn. The clouds glowed with a little orange. He turned back to Larilyn. She looked down and was breathing deeply. He caressed her ear again.

"It was a bad dream," he said.

She nodded a bit, took his hand and got up.

The two rode into the first streaks of the morning light, the songbirds greeting them with their music. The western mountains were to their left and they could see the snow-capped peaks. A cool breeze was meeting them head-on from the north. The two later slowed down into a trot to let the horses rest a bit. Larilyn pulled out some nuts and tore off a bit of bread.

"Want some breakfast?" she asked her husband. Orilin pulled up to her.

"Sure." Orilin took a bit of the nuts and a handful of bread. They ate slowly as they gazed into the rising sun. Larilyn shared the water skin with him.

"Do you really think there is any real danger on the way we are going?" she asked Orilin. He shrugged.

"I wouldn't think so. If other bits of the Flame are out also, it would be in places like Caltirion, I imagine. But we are still days away from getting there."

"So what is that supposed to mean?"

"Well," said Orilin. "If the Flame is going out around the world, I would suspect the panicking is going on in places like Caltirion; where bits of the Flame are. The place I'm really worried about is Al-Nartha. There could be an all-out riot."

"And accusations."

"Precisely," said Orilin. "I know right now I'm struggling for words, but I'm having difficulty understanding all of this. Never in the history of the world that I know of has the Flame diminished."

"Maybe Elimed also had a point about the Meldron," said Larilyn. Orilin turned around in his saddle and looked at her.

"In what way?"

"Well," she said, "They are the ones who wanted to put the Flame out anyway. They are the ones who have the doctrines of blackness and search after the so-called Eternal Secret."

Orilin thought over this for a second.

"I'm sure there is more about that in the Chronicles of the Vicars of Laerdiron, isn't there?" he asked.

"Heh!" chuckled Larilyn. "I don't know. You're the one who studied under Elrad."

Orilin thought a bit. He went through the account of the confrontation with Cyrus and Ralharin in his mind; of the first dissension between Elf and Meldron.

"Well," he said. "There was a threat that Ralharin made to Cyrus. Something about the Flame being idolatry. Something also about foretelling snuffing the Flame out. The Meldron do dabble in augury, but I don't see how that can extinguish the Flame. The Creator made the Flame, and all of Telbyrin came forth from it. How could augury thwart the power of the Creator?"

"I don't believe it can," replied Larilyn.

"Nor do I," said Orilin. "When we meet with Elrad I'm sure he will have a better idea."

Larilyn nodded. They rode on in silence for a while.

"I hope that Arch Vicar Hhrin-Calin will know what to do," said Larilyn.

Orilin nodded.

"He should."

"By the way you have spoken of him, I always thought Elrad would have been Arch Vicar," said Larilyn.

"I did too," said Orilin. "Elrad ordained Hhrin-Calin, and Lyrinias really favored him."

"You and Lyrinias developed a great friendship," she said, "Practically like brothers. With Lyrinias, Elrad, Hhrin-Calin and yourself, this riddle can be solved, don't you think?"

Orilin closed his eyes and then looked toward the north.

"I don't know if any Human or Elf can, love. But we will try." Larilyn then trotted up beside him.

"Hah," she sighed. "I guess our peaceful life on the farm is over. It's back to Caltirion."

Orilin shook his head and smiled.

"Don't say that too quickly, love. As soon is this thing is over, if I have anything to say about it, were going back to that farm."

"If it gets over," Larilyn sighed.

Orilin took her hand and looked at her. The horses stopped.

"Don't worry," he said. "The mountains themselves can crumble and the sun can darken. I will not leave you nor give up on this. We can have our dream."

Larilyn smiled and squeezed his hand.

"You really think so?" she asked.

Orilin nodded.

"Yes." She smiled.

The two rode on for another day living off of the bread, cheese and nuts. It was a lot of riding and they were getting tired.

"We better start looking for a settlement soon," said Larilyn.

"Not liking the open sky and the bare earth?" asked Orilin.

"Well," she said. "I'm dirty and need a bath. You do too. We need to find a settlement."

"There are no towns between here and the Dreath Wood."

"Yes, but there are hamlets," she said. "Bath. Food. Soon!"

Orilin laughed a bit.

"Yes, ma'am." He was glad she was feeling better and things were lightening up for them and becoming amusing. They had been through a lot during the past few days.

They rode until mid-afternoon and indeed ran across a small hamlet. It was gently spaced out and looked welcoming. A guard tower was up ahead and one guard was stationed.

"Who are you and what do you want?"

Orilin and Larilyn looked at each other and grinned.

"We want the best establishment you got," said Orilin. "And a place for the horses. We are tired. Good food and a …"

"This isn't Acaida, Elf," barked the guard. "Nothing here but a very small tavern. But, if you have enough gold, I'll take you to Madam Tarra's place. She is nice to travelers."

"Why does Madam Tarra need gold to be nice to travelers?" asked Orilin.

"What?" asked the guard. "You think good looks and a nice grin get you what you want? Not here, Elf."

"My name is Orilin," he said. "And I'd like to meet this Madam Tarra. That is, if she has good pies." The guard shook his head.

"Come on in. Let me check you first." The two Elves came through the inspection and went into the hamlet. It was naturally a settlement of Humans and was a community of farmers and homesteaders. People went by and tipped hats and waved to the Elves.

"Nice people," said Larilyn. Two little children ran up to the horses.

"Elves!" they said. "Please play us a song!"

Larilyn smiled and pulled out her pipes, as did Orilin. They rode past the children playing another little duet. The children clapped and cheered.

The guard was leading them. He took them past little shops such as a carpenter and blacksmith. There was a little warm-looking house on a knoll just ahead.

"There," said the guard. "That's her home. Be nice to her. She is a widow. That will be two gold pieces. Sargnan currency."

"What!?" said Orilin. "That's highway robbery! You want two gold pieces just for leading us to a house?"

"Two," said the guard. "Or I put you out."

Orilin narrowed his gaze.

"You and what army?"

Larilyn lay a hand on his arm.

"Please, sir, we don't want any trouble," she said. "We are but poor Elves, poor cattle farmers. Why, we can barely able feed ourselves with …"

"All right, all right," he said. "One gold piece, and that's just because you're pretty."

Larilyn cocked her head.

"Why, thank you good sir." She winked and smiled at him. Orilin was scowling. Larilyn handed the guard the gold piece and they rode on.

"Well, you handled that nicely," said Orilin. "Apparently good looks and a nice grin get you what you want in this place after all."

Larilyn laughed a haughty laugh.

"It's in the eyes, love."

Orilin smirked.

They reached the cozy little home after they had ridden up the knoll. A light was lit inside, and the door handle opened. The figure inside the home was not what Orilin was expecting. She was a Human about in her mid-forties. She had closely cropped brown hair and hazel eyes. Orilin was expecting a plump little woman in a bonnet with a pie in her hands to greet them.

"You must be Madam Tarra," said Larilyn.

The woman nodded.

"I am. What are your names?"

"I'm Larilyn Alandiron. This is my husband, Orilin Alandiron."

The woman cocked her head a bit and narrowed her gaze.

"Seems like I should know that name," she said. "Sounds very … I don't know. Well, come in. Let me tie up your horses."

The two Elves thanked her and tied up their horses to an outside post. Madam Tarra walked around the house.

"Follow me. Let's water your animals."

Orilin and Madam Tarra grabbed two buckets and filled them up at her well. They then brought them back to the horses who were grateful to receive it. Madam Tarra even fed them some hay.

"Come in," she said. "Do you need something to eat?" Orilin looked at her a bit nervously.

"Well, we have been traveling a long time."

"What's your destination," asked Madam Tarra.

"Caltirion."

Madam Tarra's eyes narrowed again.

"Long way," she said. "Are you saying that you need a place to stay?"

"Aaa," said Orilin.

"Don't worry about it," she said. "I can put you up for one night. I actually enjoy the company. And I certainly don't get to see Elves that often. Come in."

Orilin and Larilyn looked at each other and nodded. The house they entered was beautifully decorated. There were paintings on the wall of Madam Tarra and a man beside her whom the Elves could only imagine was her deceased husband. There were scented candles and a fireplace which was not lit. The springtime weather was too warm for a fire.

"I'm about to start dinner," she said. "How does bean

soup sound? I'm sorry I cannot offer you more but I was not expecting you."

"That's fine," said Orilin.

As Madam Tarra prepared the soup, she hummed a soft song. The two Elves continued to look around the house.

"If you want to move your things in," she said, "You can do so. There is an extra bedroom in the back."

Larilyn went up to her.

"Is there a place outside of town where I could bathe? I don't want to …"

"Just let me heat you up some water and you can bathe all you want to here. I'll start the fire to warm the water."

Larilyn smiled.

"Thank you, Madam," she said.

Orilin volunteered instead to start the fire. It wasn't long until he had a fire going. As the fire burned, the coals gathered and Madam Tarra and Orilin put the pot full of water on the coals. It took a while for the water to heat. Orilin carried the warm water to his wife.

When he walked back into the kitchen, Madam Tarra was still working on the bean soup and bread. He paced around a bit. He wanted to ask her something specific but didn't know how to word it.

"How long have you lived here, Madam?" he asked. She looked up briefly from her cooking.

"I've lived in this settlement since I married Derran. He died three years ago."

Orilin nodded.

"I'm sorry."

Tarra sighed.

"It was inevitable."

Orilin was not going to ask how Derran died. He paced around a bit more.

"Madam, have you noticed anything untoward or odd recently?"

Tarra looked at him.

"Why do you ask?"

Orilin thought about how he was going to answer that.

"Well, something happened in Acaida a few days ago. Something odd."

"Like what?" she asked.

"Well, we think someone is involved with something sinister. Something odd," said Orilin evading the question. "Someone caused a disturbance in Acaida."

"Well, whoever did it should have to answer to the constable," said Tarra. "Isn't that what happened?"

"I don't know," said Orilin. "I just want know if anyone has been causing trouble in this settlement."

"Not that I know of," said Tarra. "Are you a constable, Mr. Orilin?" Orilin shook his head. He couldn't evade the question anymore. He knew he wasn't good at it.

"No," he said. "I was once a member of the Lorinthian Guard in Caltirion."

"And what do you do now?" she asked.

"I'm a farmhand. Life is a lot simpler now."

"I bet," said Tarra. "Why did you leave the Guard?"

Orilin sighed, relieved that the subject was changed without having to go into the detail about the Flame.

"I wanted a life without violence. I met Larilyn then."

Tarra smiled.

"Nice," she said. "How long have you been working on the farm?"

"A couple of years," he said. "Larilyn has worked there even longer."

"So you met her on the farm? How nice."

Orilin and Tarra continued to make small talk and Larilyn emerged from the bathroom all clean; her hair still damp.

"That feels so much better," she said. Orilin smiled and looked around again. He knew he was going to have to move around the hamlet that night; perhaps go to the tavern to find out more information. Taverns were where people talked.

"Dinner is served," said Tarra. The three sat down to the simple hot meal. A dessert was even served. Blueberry pie. Orilin was very pleased.

Chapter 5

LARILYN MADE ORILIN BATHE AFTER SUPPER WHILE SHE and Madam Tarra cleaned up. He had to admit, the bath was rather nice. When he was done, he dried off and put back on his clothes. After he had emptied out the bath water, he went to the bedroom.

"You smell better," said Larilyn sleepily.

Orilin smirked.

"Thanks."

Larilyn propped her head up on one hand.

"Will you play me to sleep?" she asked looking toward his harp.

"Of course, my little cow-punch."

Larilyn laid back on the bed.

"This bed is so nice," she said.

"Enjoy it while you can," Orilin replied.

"Mmm," said Larilyn as she laid her head on the pillow. Orilin picked up his harp and strummed a little.

"Love, I need to go down to the tavern later."

Larilyn looked up.

"What for? We had that muscadine wine."

"I want to know what people are talking about. Sorry.

I need to investigate."

"Whatever," she groaned as she snuggled back into the pillow. "You have to play me to sleep first. And don't stay away from me long."

Orilin laughed.

"I won't."

He played a playful tune that was yet gentle, gleeful and light. It wasn't long until she was asleep.

ϒϒϒϒϒϒ

Orilin went out into the night carrying nothing but a few coins and his pipes. Going to this place was a necessary evil. He didn't want to spend all night there. He walked down a dusty road dimly lit by the little houses. It was where that thief of a guard led them to Madam Tarra's.

He came to an inviting tavern that had a sign simply of a beer mug. Orilin went in and saw many men there – all respectable looking; no drunken rabble. The men were either drinking or smoking pipes. Fiddle music and a couple of men singing were in the background. They were singing something of a ghost story and a few men, farmers mostly, were listening intently. One man, wearing a green vest trimmed with gold, sat up and looked to Orilin.

"Sit down with us, lad," he said. "Can we get you something to drink?" Orilin went over to the table with the men and pulled up a chair.

"My, people are nice in this town," he said. "What is your name, good sir?"

"Janton," he said. "What will you have?" Orilin looked around and then back at the man.

"Just a beer. Good and stout."

"You'll want to try the Acaida ale," he said.

Orilin smiled.

"It is one of my favorites."

The beer was served, and Orilin took a long drought.

"Where are you from?" asked Janton. "We don't get a

whole lot of travelers here."

"We are from a small farm about two days from Acaida."

"We? Who else is with you?"

"My wife and I," said Orilin. "We are heading north to Caltirion." Some of the men's eyes widened.

"That's quite a ways," said Janton. "What, I may ask, takes you to Caltirion?"

"I have friends there," said Orilin. "It's been years since I've seen them. And we have very important business."

"Hmm," said Janton. "No Pilgrimage for you and your wife?" Orilin was hoping he was not going to ask that question. He felt awkward.

"Well … ah we really were pressed for time this year. We said our prayers this year in the Sanctuary of Acaida. It's where we were married. It was nice."

"Ah," said Janton. "Indeed not everyone can afford to go to Al-Nartha every year. Especially poor farmers, eh?"

"Yeah," said Orilin. "Especially poor farmers." Oh, he was hoping they were not going to ask any more prying questions. Luckily, the rest of the men were too interested in their beer and pipes. Hopefully, his story was convincing.

"You just watch out, young one," said another one of the men. "There have been reports of Barras Drin and his horde north of here."

Orilin was shocked.

"Barras Drin?! Coming south?"

"Yes," said the old man.

"You may want to consider going back to where you came from," said Janton.

"Our business is too important for that," said Orilin.

"Must be pretty important business," said Janton. "If you know how to evade Barras Drin, you'll be all right. Folks around here are getting a little anxious too."

"How long have you known about this?" asked Orilin.

"Since yesterday," said the other man.

Orilin and the Lorinthian Guard had had dealings with Barras Drin before. He and his horde were probably the most notorious outlaws in Telbyrin; and they knew who Orilin Alandiron was. He could not risk it; he and Larilyn could not deal with them. Their only option was to go through the Dreath Wood, and he had been hoping very much that they could avoid that.

"Tell me, gentlemen," said Orilin. "Are there any more odd happenings in the world these days?" Janton narrowed his eyes and took a long drag on his pipe.

"Well," said Janton, "Besides for the bandits up north, nothing much." Orilin was happy, yet disappointed in some ways. These people were clueless. They had no idea what was going on in the world right now. Orilin finished his ale in one long draught and put it down on the table. He put out a couple of copper coins.

"Oh, no," said Janton. "It's on us. Do you have to leave so soon?"

Orilin knew it would look odd if he left so quickly.

"Well," he said. "I guess I have time for another." The men cheered.

ϓ ϓ ϓ ϓ ϓ ϓ

Orilin stayed at the tavern for about another half hour. He talked much with Janton and his friends; small talk mainly, but no more news he could use for their journey. He was very grateful learning about Barras Drin.

He soon bid the men goodbye and walked back up the path toward Madam Tarra's house. Many of the houses had already snuffed their candles out for the night. Only the light from a half-moon and the stars gave sufficient light. He reached Madam Tarra's and gently knocked. He saw a candle lit deep within another room and come toward him. Madam Tarra opened the door.

"Hmm," she said. "You didn't stay that long."

Orilin smirked.

"Just a bunch of old men and their pipes."

Madam Tarra laughed a little.

"Come on in," she said. Orilin walked in. Madam Tarra closed the door and looked back at him.

"Will you need anything else tonight, Mr. Orilin?"

"Just a good night's sleep," he said.

She smiled.

"Your wife sleeps well," she said. "Goodnight, Mr. Orilin."

Madam Tarra and the candle proceeded to the back room. Orilin went back to his bedroom.

It was totally dark when he walked in. He heard the gentle breathing of his wife as she slept. Careful not to wake her, he pulled off his boots, sat down, and looked out the window. What were they going to do? Was he going to brave Barras Drin or the Dreath Wood? Neither place he wanted to take his wife to. There was a stirring.

"Come here," said Larilyn. He smiled. She slowly leaned up.

"What's keeps you up, love?"

Orilin turned around and sat beside her.

"I found out some things," he said. "Things are getting more complicated." Larilyn took his hand and laid her forehead on his.

"Tell me in the morning," she said.

"Love," he said. "It's going to be really dangerous."

She smiled.

"Love. I trust you. You're tired and you need to sleep." She lovingly touched one of his ears.

"How are we going to do this, Larilyn?" he sighed.

"Shhh," she whispered. "Sleep now." Orilin could not resist.

ϒ ϒ ϒ ϒ ϒ ϒ

The Elves slept late that morning. Not even the bright sunlight or the roosters crowing woke them. People outside were milling about their work and the sounds of loud voices and clinking of wagon wheels gently woke Orilin. He jumped up and pulled off the covers. Larilyn stirred.

"Mmm," she groaned and threw the covers back on her. Orilin decided not to wake her. He got up, put his boots on and went outside to where the well was. He took a pail and splashed some water on his face.

"Good morning," said Madam Tarra. Orilin turned around.

"Good morning," he said. "Sorry we slept so late. Is there anything we can help you with?" Tarra shook her head.

"No. You two get some breakfast and stay as long as you need. If you stay longer, I'll need some help with gathering the eggs. The rooster is particularly mean and stubborn."

"Fair enough," said Orilin. "I'm sorry, but after that we need to be riding on. We have important business up north. I can't thank you enough for your hospitality. Would a gold piece be sufficient?"

"Wow," remarked Tarra, "That's quite a lot. You two were really not that much trouble. Five copper to replace the food is quite enough."

He was hesitant to pay such a nice woman so little. He and Larilyn had been treated like royalty.

"Five copper then," he said, "Though I feel a bit guilty for paying you so little."

Tarra shook her head.

"No worries. You and your wife have a safe journey. May the Creator bless you both."

Orilin bid her the same blessing.

He went back into the house and prepared a little breakfast for Larilyn. She was lying in bed with her mouth open making a funny noise. Orilin laughed a little at this.

"Come on, little farm girl," he whispered, "Time to get up." Her mouth closed and she woke. Her hair was disheveled and she yawned and rubbed her eyes.

"Oh," she remarked. "What time is it?"

"It's mid-morning," he said. "We need to eat and ride."

"Agh. I was hoping … well … we do need to be riding." Orilin smiled. He was glad her morale was up.

"Ah," she said with surprise, "Breakfast." Orilin hand-ed the bread, cheese, fruit and an egg on the board to her. He got her some water.

"Go ahead and take your time," he said. "I'll go pack." Larilyn nodded.

Orilin started to pack when heard some commotion outside the window. Some men talking loudly about some-thing. Orilin's curiosity was piqued and he went over to the window.

"Barras Drin is north and may be riding south. What's he doing in these parts? We are totally undefended."

"We'll have to call every able-bodied man to arms then," said another. "We can't just sit here." The other men scoffed.

"What do you think we can do against his horde? You're as mad as they say."

"How far are they out?"

"I don't know. They could be two or three days for all I know." Orilin's blood stirred. They had to get out of here.

"Larilyn, as soon as you finish, we need to ride." She looked at him strangely.

"What's going on?"

"You didn't hear outside?"

"No. What is it?"

"Barras Drin." Larilyn dropped her piece of bread.

"Barras Drin! Here?!" Orilin's lips pursed.

"Could be soon. We need to ride." Larilyn got ready as fast as she could.

"I can't believe this," she said. "This may be just the talk of old men, Orilin."

"Could be," he said. "Could not be. Either way, I'm seeing us to safety."

The two bade a hasty goodbye to Madam Tarra and loaded up their horses. They were well-fed and watered. They did decide to tell Madam Tarra of the potential danger since she was going to hear of it anyway.

"Be careful," said Orilin. "See the people somewhere safe."

"If our time has come then it has come," she said. "We might have to …"

"Try to avoid that," said Orilin. "Weapons are not the answer. Your people will be destroyed. If they come they will put your people under their rule. Send someone to ride to Acaida. If they are truly coming south it will be in danger as well."

"What will you do, Mr. Orilin?"

"I'll ride as hard as I can to Gallinthrar. Hopefully their cavalry is defending south Hallintor. But Acaida's cavalry have a duty to protect north Sargna. That's about all I can do. Perhaps I can persuade Gallinthrar to continue to distract them."

Madam Tarra nodded.

"Don't you worry about us," she said. "You take care."

Orilin nodded. He spurred his horse and Larilyn followed, riding due north with the people moving as they went.

Chapter 6

ORILIN AND LARILYN RODE AT A FAST PACE sweeping through fields of sage and fescue. The western mountains still loomed in the distance.

"How much farther to the forest?" asked Larilyn.

Orilin looked back.

"We should reach there by nightfall, though we need to try to go around it."

Larilyn rode up beside him.

"What if the horde is there?" Orilin shook his head.

"They won't go there. They are just as uneasy about it as we are."

Larilyn narrowed her gaze. She saw it first.

"Orilin, look." He looked ahead and saw it. There were black clouds looming on the far distant horizon. Flashes of lightning could be seen among them.

"A storm," Larilyn said. "And a bad one at that. We need to find shelter."

"It's still a ways out," said Orilin. "Let's ride hard and water the horses at the next stream." The Elves spurred the flanks of their horses, and they increased into a quick gallop. The plains were level as they rode on.

They rode for a while more until they did reach a small spring and stopped to let the horses drink their fill. Orilin pulled out their water skin and he and his wife drank from it. The sky above them was still blue, but the storm in the distance was getting closer. Soon the whole sky would be cloudy.

"Now we need to be seeking that shelter of yours, love," said Orilin.

Larilyn drank more from the skin and refilled it.

"I don't know where we will find one. Can we shelter just inside the wood?"

Orilin looked nervous.

"I don't think that's a good idea."

"Well, where will we shelter, love?" she asked. "The storm is upon us."

Orilin looked up. There was dust gathering along the ground below the storm. He ran up a bit farther and put his ear to the ground. He then heard it. Rumbling. Not of lighting, but of horses' hooves.

"Orilin!" shouted Larilyn. "Come here!" He ran back and knelt beside the spring.

"It's the horde," he said.

Larilyn's eyes widened.

"Then we have to go to the wood," she said. Orilin shook his head.

"We have to avoid that wood, Larilyn." She took him by the shoulders.

"You cannot fight them by yourself, love," she said strongly. "We have to hide. Don't be afraid of these spirits."

Orilin looked down and slowly nodded.

"All right," he said. "But you are not to leave my side for any reason. Understand?"

Larilyn looked at him and nodded.

"Okay," said Orilin. "We take the road to the wood. But we will only stay concealed until they pass."

Larilyn nodded again.

They shifted their traveling slightly to the left. Orilin had been to Janlar before and he never wanted to go again.

But this time he had no choice. The sky was blackening and the lightning was getting brighter. Larilyn felt a few drops of water hit her face.

"It will be raining soon," she said.

"I hope it slows them down," replied Orilin. The dust in the distance was getting thicker.

Then they saw it. It was a blackening in the distance. The Dreath Wood. Orilin and Larilyn spurred the horses on until they sprinted.

"We're almost there," shouted Orilin as a flash of lightning darted across the sky. The thunder was loud and seemed to shake the earth.

"Hyah!" yelled Larilyn. The horses kept sprinting up to the wood. The lightning was getting even more violent. Orilin jumped off his horse and quickly tied it up to the nearest tree. He helped Larilyn off hers and they tied her horse beside his.

"They are exhausted," she said.

"We may have to leave them," said Orilin.

"Leave them?!"

"The horde cannot follow us into the forest, Larilyn. The horses might give us away." He jumped up a little knoll and ran up the top of a hill. The trees were blowing as Orilin looked out over the distance. He could start to make out shapes of men riding.

"They are coming straight ahead," he said. "Let the horses go, dear!"

"Orilin! Why…"

"Now, love!" Larilyn looked around frantically, gathered their meager belongings off the animals and slapped them on the hindquarters.

"Hyah!" she yelled. The horses neighed and galloped off into the distance. Orilin ran down to his wife. The two took hands and ran into the woods.

ᵧᵧᵧᵧᵧᵧ

They had hidden under a small hill with a bog under it.

The two sat beside the bog on wet loamy soil. The storm was fully upon them. There was very little rain; just strong gusts of wind and more strong lightning. The two Elves could hear the riders thundering past the wood. There were probably more than 50 of them, Orilin estimated.

"I have to go look," he said to his wife.

"What?!" she whispered. "You stay right here!" Orilin touched one of her ears.

"I'll be right back," he promised. Taking his sword, he clambered up the hill a bit. The horses were slowing down a bit. Orilin ran fast and hid behind a large oak. He could now hear voices.

"Whoa! Yah!" yelled many of the riders. There was a small silence.

"Why are we stopping, Umbra?" said one voice. "This place is accursed."

"Only because they failed the test, Barras," said a female voice. "Horses have run ahead of us."

Orilin peered from around the oak to see between the trees a man with jet black flowing hair and tanned skin. Sitting beside him was a woman clothed in a large grey cloak with a hood drawn over her head. She hopped off her horse and tossed her cowl off. She was grey skinned, had long black hair, yellowish eyes and pointed ears almost like an Elf's. The fierce wind whipped her hair all around as she held the pommel of her sword at her waist.

"This forest has visitors," she said.

"Don't do it, Umbra," said the man beside her. She turned around.

"I live in the darkness, Barras," she replied. "I am not afraid of these spirits of Janlar. Not just anyone visits the Dreath Wood. If this forest has Vicars hiding in it, I will not see them get away!" Orilin turned around in horror. The woman was a Meldron. This was getting much worse. He crawled back to Larilyn waiting for him by the bog.

"It's Barras Drin," he whispered to her. "And he is accompanied by a Meldron guide."

"What?!," whispered Larilyn.

"Shhh," he whispered. "Don't move."

The Meldron woman moved into the forest clearing brambles and brush away with her sword. She stopped and sniffed the air. The dark man on the horse followed her in.

"There is no one here, Umbra. Let's be moving on." Meanwhile Orilin's grip on his sword tightened. Larilyn was getting even more afraid. Flashbacks of the dream she had the other night haunted her. The Elven couple was in her mind.

"Stay back!" the Elf woman in the dream hissed. The darkness enveloped her mind. Meanwhile the Meldron woman walked further into the forest. She sniffed the air again.

"He is not here," she said quietly.

The dark man smirked.

"He never was. Because he knows in this place he would die. This place is death, Umbra."

The woman looked back at him.

"We ride south. The men of Menetarra are riding north and my scouts continue to ride south. Menetarra will deal with Gallinthrar."

The dark man smirked again and nodded. Orilin and Larilyn could hear the men and the Meldron woman getting back on their horses. They started to gallop away. It was now starting to get dark. Orilin crawled up the hill a bit to watch them ride off. He watched until the last horse went out of his sight. Larilyn was crawling up the hill a bit and kneeled next to her husband.

"What was all that talk about Menetarra?"

"I don't know," said Orilin. "If the Menetarrans are riding this way and they are heading towards Gallinthrar then it sounds like Elimed was right; there might be war. But Barras Drin and this Meldron woman are looking for someone. They mentioned a "he," whoever "he" is. There was also something about the Vicars hiding."

"Where could they be hiding?" asked Larilyn.

"I don't know," replied Orilin. "It's too early to tell. We have to head towards Gallinthrar. From there we go to Caltirion. So much for our plan on getting Gallinthrar to distract

Barras Drin. They now will have plenty to deal with regarding the Menetarrans."

"Caltirion does also," added Larilyn. Orilin nodded.

"Probably so. The Meldron woman mentioned scouts riding south. We will have to stay concealed. North through these woods leads to Gallinthrar. We will have to take woods."

Larilyn nodded glumly.

Orilin looked at her and took her shoulders.

"Remember, never leave my side. In fact, never let go of my hand. If you see something strange, ignore it. Kharlia has many spirits. Don't let go."

"I won't, love," she said.

"Okay," he replied. "We can sleep here on this hill tonight. In the morning we can start through the wood. We never travel through the wood at night."

$$\Upsilon \, \Upsilon \, \Upsilon \, \Upsilon \, \Upsilon \, \Upsilon$$

The night's sleep was fitful. Screech owls could be heard in the distance as well as the crickets. Larilyn never left her husband's side. Orilin stayed awake most of the night watching for anything. It was only so long that he could hold out awake. Sleep overtook him, but he had his sword laid next to him.

When morning finally came it was still dark and cloudy. The storm had not fully passed. Orilin shook his wife gently on the shoulder.

"Larilyn," he whispered. She groaned a little and then turned over.

"We have to be moving," he said. "Let's go." The two picked up their belongings and headed on down the trail. Larilyn reached into the rucksack to grab a few nuts and handed some to her husband. The two munched on them a bit and drank some water.

"Better conserve the rest," said Larilyn. "In case we get lost."

"We can't get lost," said Orilin nervously. The two continued down a clearing onto another stream and they did not see any wildlife. Not a deer or another mammal in sight. There were a few bottom-feeding fish in the stream. The side of the stream was overgrown with weeds and brambles. Orilin hopped over the stream and helped his wife across. The two continued to follow the stream.

At midday there was still no sun – only dark clouds. The Elves stopped for a quick bite of bread which they had rationed. Their water skin was about three-quarters full. Larilyn looked ahead.

"How much farther?"

"We are nearing the ancient battle sights of Janlar," said Orilin. "From now on be extra careful. If you see something out of the ordinary, don't pay it any attention. Try not to look … just stay by me."

"Okay," she whispered.

The two walked through an opening of many ferns that grew next to the little stream. The wood was getting dark and thick. A bit of dry wind blew past them. Larilyn stepped on something. It was hard and rough. Her foot slipped off of it a bit and she looked down. It was a helmet, all rusted, which looked like it had lain there for many a year.

"Orilin," she said. He looked back.

"I know," he replied. "We are on the battlegrounds. Let's keep moving."

They kept walking through the ferns and followed the river down farther. Even though it was midday it was still getting darker in the wood. They crossed over another hill and went down into an area where the stream had turned into other bogs and sludge.

Then they saw it: the battlefields. There were dried bones everywhere and other pieces of armor. Rusted weapons lay around. There was a skull incased in one of the helmets. Larilyn looked at it. It was just there; but a horrid sight nonetheless.

"What happened here?" asked Larilyn.

"There was a battle between Gallinthrar and a rebel

named Kharlia. She led her rebel group to this spot to ambush the lord of Gallinthrar."

"What were they fighting about?" she asked.

"Gallinthrar took slaves of boys from Kharlia's village here in this forest to become soldiers in the lord's army. They were overall oppressing the villages severely. This all led up to the lord of Gallinthrar taking Kharlia's daughter to become the bride of his son. This is what led to the rebellion. Kharlia thought they would ambush the forces of Gallinthrar here, but it was not much of an ambush. Kharlia's rebels killed a few of them, but the ones who survived easily destroyed the rebels. They took Kharlia hostage."

"What did they do?" asked Larilyn.

"They blinded her. They doomed her to walk forever in this wood, grieving over her loss and her rebellion against Gallinthrar, experiencing all but seeing nothing." Larilyn picked up her pace with her husband.

"Didn't Caltirion step in?"

Orilin shook his head.

"This was a feud between a lord of Gallinthrar and his villages. Gallinthrar had rights as its own city-state and still does, as you know. We can't speak any more of this. This tale is a tale of woe; she haunts this place and people are lost here still."

"What … happens to them?" she whispered.

Orilin looked back at her.

"They are blinded."

Larilyn shuddered.

"We have to keep moving," said Orilin. "Let us not stare at anything." They made another round on the path by the bogs. They could see skulls above and below the surface of the bogs. Pieces of armor and more helmets were scattered about. They made a path up another hill where there were many large oak trees. Larilyn could make out something swinging from them; she did not know what it was. Orilin tried to keep his eyes fixed on the path they were walking on. Then they saw the hideous items that were swinging from the trees. They were skeletons with the nooses still around their necks.

"Orilin!" Larilyn said in horror. He squeezed her hand.

"Don't look!" he said. One skeleton swinging brushed Larilyn's hair. She jumped back. Orilin picked up the pace.

"We have to hurry through here."

"Why has no one given these people a proper burial?" asked Larilyn.

"They are too afraid of her," said Orilin.

Suddenly they saw a huge oak. They were approaching it fast. There was a hand that jutted out from the oak. Orilin was the first to see it. He looked again, and the hand went back behind the tree. His breathing increased.

"We have to run," he said. The two Elves started to run as a figure emerged from behind the huge oak. It was a woman clothed in white, but stained all in blood. She lifted her long blond tresses and revealed her face. There were no eyes to be found. She stumbled toward them.

"Give me your eyes so that I can see," she hissed at Orilin. She lifted up her bony fingers which had claws for fingernails.

"Give me your eyes!" she said again.

Orilin unsheathed his sword.

"Stay back, Kharlia!" he yelled. The woman was startled a bit. She stumbled closer. Orilin pushed Larilyn behind him.

"Don't look at her," he said.

"Give me them so that I may find my daughter," said the ghoul. "Give them to me!" Orilin swung his sword through the woman's body. There was a hissing sound as the blade passed through. Kharlia cackled at them.

"I'm already dead," she said. "You cannot kill me again."

Orilin didn't know what else to do.

"Run, Larilyn!" he yelled. The two Elves tried to run but Kharlia caught Orilin's boot with her bony hands.

"Give me your eyes!" she screamed. Orilin fell to the ground dropping his sword. Larilyn turned around at a distance.

"Orilin!" she screamed. She didn't know what to do. She reached for a large branch, picked one up and ran toward the specter attempting to hit it across the head. Just then there was a bright flash, and Kharlia shrieked.

"Begone, ghoul!" commanded a booming voice. There was a figure in a white and gold robe. He was holding a bit of the Flame in his hands above his head. Kharlia shrieked again, stumbled up and bounded back into the wood.

Orilin looked up to see the figure and the Flame. He couldn't believe it. Apparently, some bits of the Flame were still alive. He got up and ran to his wife. The two embraced and then looked to the figure holding the Flame. He was an Elf; dark skinned with a short white beard.

"Thank you," said Orilin. Larilyn said the same.

"Why is so young a couple gallivanting through the Dreath Wood?" he asked.

"We are on our way to Caltirion," said Orilin. "There is trouble on the plains so we decided to take the wood. It is foolish, I know, but we had to do it. You are a Vicar, I see."

The Elf nodded.

"I am. And I will lead you out of here." Orilin picked up his sword and sheathed it. They looked again at the bit of the Flame in the Vicar's hand.

"We should say a prayer of thanksgiving," said Larilyn. Orilin nodded and they said a prayer of thanksgiving for deliverance.

"We don't have much time," said the Vicar. "She will be back. Follow me." Orilin and Larilyn followed the Vicar down a small ravine.

"What is your name, sir," asked Orilin.

The Vicar looked back.

"I'm called Raltaron," he said. "And you?"

"Orilin Alandiron," he said. "This is my wife, Larilyn."

The Vicar nodded.

"I've heard about you, Orilin," he said. "Lyrinias speaks highly of you."

Orilin shook his head.

"Do you have business in Caltirion as well?"

The Vicar smirked.

"I have very important business."

"Then perhaps we can travel with you," said Orilin. "We are coming from Acaida. The Flame has gone out there."

"As it has in a lot of places," said Raltaron. "I was hiding here until the storm passed."

"Where are you coming from?" asked Orilin.

"From the Airell Mountains. From the Western Enclave. The Flame has not gone out there. Elrad rode to us with this emergency and we are going to speak to the Arch Vicar when he arrives this month. Caltirion cannot afford to see chaos."

"Then do you know about …"

"I do know about the Meldron sorceress riding south of here with Barras Drin. That was who I was hiding from here. So I guess I'm as guilty as you are seeking refuge in this forest. But I suppose that's the best we can do for now, eyh?"

Orilin nodded.

"I suppose. Are you headed straight for Caltirion?"

"I am, but our paths cannot be the same."

"Why not?" asked Larilyn. "We are much safer with the Flame present with us."

"The Flame is not the Creator, girl," he said gruffly. "The Flame is a symbol of hope, and someone is trying to fizzle out hope in the world. I will travel with you as far as the edge of this wood. In Caltirion, I will see you again. Then we can continue this conversation if you like. But for now we have to hurry out of this place."

Orilin and Larilyn looked at each other.

"Lead on," said Orilin. Raltaron stopped and looked back at them.

"Your sword will be needed again, Orilin Alandiron. Elrad and King Lyrinias are now looking for you I hear. Present yourself to them and Hhrin-Calin when you arrive in Caltirion."

"I do not wish to get involved in another war," said Orilin. "If Lyrinias and Elrad need me, I don't mind helping, but I don't want to do it with a sword."

"How you will help us is not up to you," said Raltaron. "If the Flame is going out and a Meldron sorceress is summoning hordes from the north there may be war. Like I said, Caltirion cannot afford to see chaos with the Flame out. It is still the bastion of Hallintor and of Humankind. Understand?"

Orilin slowly nodded.

"Why does Caltirion so desperately need me? I and Larilyn have done our part. We were traveling to Caltirion to tell them of the Flame. But you are bringing a piece of the Flame there I see."

"I am," said Raltaron. "And I do not know where else it has gone out. You must continue your journey to Caltirion."

"I'm a farmer now, Raltaron. Both me and my wife."

"Probably not anymore," he replied.

Chapter 7

RALTARON LED THEM THROUGH A QUICK EXIT OUT of the Dreath Wood. They were both glad to have left it. It was night by then. The moon was full and the skies were a bit cloudy. Ethlaharin shone bright in the northeast. They walked in silence for a long time.

"What exactly is going on with the Flame?" asked Orilin. Raltaron kept walking.

"I told you we can continue this conversation in Caltirion," he said.

"I was trying to help by relaying the message to Elrad and Lyrinias," said Orilin.

"They already know."

"Then what do they need us for?" asked Orilin. Raltaron stopped and turned around.

"Are you always this stubborn, boy?" he asked. There was a silence. He looked to Larilyn.

"Is he?"

Larilyn looked back at him.

"No."

"Then what is the problem? Elrad and Lyrinias are my friends as well, and I will honor their wish. You, Orilin Alandiron are a Lorinthian Guard."

"Was one!" replied Orilin.

Raltaron gritted his teeth.

"You are being re-summoned then."

Orilin shook his head.

"I can only be summoned by the king of Caltirion for that!"

"Then to the king of Caltirion you must go!" barked Raltaron. "Elrad raised you as a son, did he not? And Lyrinias is like a brother to you, is he not? I'm not in the dark about this as you might think. Most likely, your farm life in Sargna is over, so get over it!"

Orilin stared at Raltaron with an icy glare.

"How can I trust your word? I don't even know you," he said.

"Well you do now!" said Raltaron. "Get going! I will see you a few days hence in Caltirion."

With that, Raltaron started off on a separate road by himself; the Flame immersed in his hands.

"So you're just leaving us?" shouted Orilin.

"I am," Raltaron yelled back. "Our paths cannot be the same. Take the ferry and go up into Hallintor. Farewell!"

Orilin watched him walk away. He turned back to his wife.

"We don't know him," he said to her. "And he is the rudest Vicar I have ever met. I don't see why …" She touched his ear.

"Calm down, love," she said. "I know you don't much care for him or for this, and I really don't either. But I do trust you. And I know you want to do the right thing. I also know you wouldn't just refuse to go back if there is the possibility that someone needs your help. But either way, love, if you go north, I go north. If you go south, I go south."

Orilin was a little stunned by his wife's words. There was a moment of silence as he held her hands.

"What do you want to do?" he asked her. She looked him in the eyes.

"I want to be with you," she said. "Wherever that road

takes. The Flame may go out, love, but I cannot believe that means the Creator has forsaken us. There are higher forces in the universe than the Flame. And I have to believe they are at work even at this time in the world. I'll follow you to Caltirion, Orilin. I'll follow you to the Mountains of Black. I trust you. I love you."

Orilin breathed deeply. He kissed her and embraced her.

"I never doubted," he said. "All I want for you is to be safe." She lay her head on his shoulder.

"We're going to get through this, love," she said. "Go where you will."

He thought.

"I am afraid for the Kesstals," he said. "The Menetar-rans might be in Sargna by now."

"We, unfortunately, can't do anything about that now, love," said Larilyn. "I only hope that they are with Elimed."

"Acaida's army can only hold out for so long," he said.

She looked up at him.

"What do you think is best?" she asked.

Orilin continued to think.

"I wish I could go back to the Kesstals and make sure that they are safe. But if Lyrinias and Elrad need me, I would like to go to them as well. We may be doing more good to help summon Caltirion and Gallinthrar's help to aid Sargna."

Larilyn lay her head back on his shoulder.

"Then what do you think?"

Orilin sighed.

"Let's get going. To Caltirion."

"To Caltirion, then," she said.

The night was clearing a bit. They found the dirt road that would lead to the ferry. The ferry itself was about three miles away or so.

"Should we walk at night?" asked Larilyn.

Orilin thought about that.

"We might as well. It's not far. The ferry will carry us to the town of Cedar Grove. It's a nice place. We can stop there for a break before we go to Caltirion. That will give us a chance to catch up on some sleep and re-supply."

"Sounds good," she said as she drank from the water skin. "I've heard of this Cedar Grove. Isn't that the place where Orinda Hallison visits a lot?"

"She practically lives there," said Orilin as they walked.

"It will be nice to hear her sing and play."

"She has a beautiful voice but she is not at all to be trusted," he replied. "She is also a very beautiful Human who has broken many an innocent man's heart. Rumor has it that she is also a bit of a pick-pocket, but that is only rumor."

Larilyn raised her eyebrows.

"That's unfortunate."

Orilin looked back.

"For whom? Her?"

"Yes," Larilyn replied. "It's a pity that she is adding to the sorry reputation of the minstrels in Gallinthrar and Caltirion."

"Those are only some of their ways, love," said Orilin. "Besides, they have another disadvantage. They do not know some of the old songs like we do. And most of their performances are done for fame, money and recognition. So your right, it's a pity."

They continued down the road, and after the long walk they saw lights in the distance. There they met the ferryman. He was a young man but clearly tired. He looked at Orilin.

"Is it just you two?" he asked.

Orilin nodded.

"Yes. What is your price?"

"Two copper," he said. "I will have you in Cedar Grove in just a bit."

The Elves boarded the ferry and paid the copper, saying nothing about the reason for their journey. The ferryman did not ask any questions either. It was late in the night and he was ready for his shift to end.

Orilin and Larilyn reached Cedar Grove in a very short time. It was a village nestled in groves of evergreen trees.

"I can see why they named it Cedar Grove," said Larilyn.

Orilin smirked.

"It's a quiet little town," he said. "I kind of like it actually."

"Even with all the corrupt minstrels," she laughed.

"Note that I said 'kind-of.'"

There was music still being played from the tavern
and inn when they walked into town. The establishment's
name was the "The Grey Fox" and it was heavily populat-
ed. The two walked into a smoke-filled room. It was about
midnight and the tables were still littered with the drunken.
The innkeeper came up to them with a look of surprise on
his face. He was a Human with a grey mustache and a grey
tunic.

"Orilin!" he said. "Good to see you, my old friend."

"Gillen," said Orilin. "You have not changed a bit, I
see."

"Yes, yes. Still running the Fox here. Who is the pretty lass beside you?"

Orilin smiled.

"This is my wife. Larilyn."

Gillen's jaw dropped.

"You got married?!"

Orilin smiled again.

"When you have found your soul-mate, Gillen, there is
no resistance."

Larilyn smiled.

"I don't understand the Elven concept of soul-mating,"
said Gillen, "but I hope it's true for us Humans too."

"I believe it is true," said Orilin. His attention was
caught to the stage. There was a Human woman dressed
in a black vest and leggings. She played a harp and sang
beautifully.

"Is that Orinda Hallison?" asked Larilyn.

Gillen nodded.

"That is her. And as long as she plays, the more business I get."

Orilin shook his head.

"The longer she plays the more drunk people get," he said.

Gillen laughed.

"Speaking of such, can I get you a drink?"

"We need a room actually," said Orilin. "And some food."

"No worries," replied Gillen. "I have some wonderful rabbit stew that Elandon made tonight. People love it."

"I'm sure people love whatever game your son brings in."

Gillen smiled.

"That's my boy."

The Elves sat down at a table.

"I'll charge you five copper for the room," said Gillen, "but the food is on the house. Enjoy."

Orilin thanked Gillen. The music over in the distance stopped and the people clapped. Orinda Hallison stepped down from the stage for a quick break. Several people tried to talk to her. She gave them the partial time of day and then went on to sit with Gillen's son, Elandon, who was basking in the attention he was getting from the seductive minstrel.

"Poor man," said Orilin. "He goes like a calf to the slaughter."

"Is she really that bad?" asked Larilyn.

"Yes," he replied. Orinda's eye caught Orilin and she smiled. Getting up from the table she went over to sit with the Elven couple. Elandon followed.

"Orilin," she said. "How nice of you to show up again. We have not seen you in over a year."

"I've been busy, Orinda," he replied.

The minstrel smiled a bit.

"With what? This Elf woman?"

"My wife, Orinda."

She chuckled.

"She is beautiful. You are a lucky man, Orilin."

"I know," he said. Larilyn blushed a little. She extended her hand to the minstrel woman.

"I'm Larilyn," she said.

65

Orinda took her hand.

"Hmm," she said. "Callouses. You're a farm girl?"

"Yes," said Larilyn. "I was raised by Bartlin and Treana Norin on an Acaida farm.

"I don't know them," said Orinda.

"They have long since passed," said Larilyn.

"I'm sure," said Orinda. "You must be old."

"I'm 300 years," she said, "Almost the same as my husband."

"And I hardly call that old, Orinda," said Orilin. The minstrel laughed.

"Compared to us, Orilin, you're both old."

The stew was brought out. It was still steaming hot. Two mugs of mead were also brought out and set beside the Elves.

"It's good to see you again, Orilin," said Elandon. "And it's nice to meet you too, Larilyn. Where are you both traveling?"

"It's personal," said Orilin.

Elandon's face went serious.

"All right."

Orilin took a bite of the stew and looked up.

"The stew is excellent, Elandon." He smiled and nodded.

"The rabbit was the plumpest I have seen in a long time."

Orinda got up from the table.

"I will leave you two to your meal," she said. "I must be getting back to the stage. Entertainment never really ceases. See you, Orilin. Perhaps I will see you two in Caltirion?"

Orilin's nerves shot up.

"Perhaps," he said. The minstrel grinned and went back to the stage. Elandon followed.

"I hope she is not in on where we are going," said Larilyn. "She is rude."

Orilin looked at his wife.

"You're catching on quick. And she does know we are

heading to Caltirion. But there is nothing we can do about that now. Just be careful what you tell her."

"I don't trust her," said Larilyn.

"I don't trust her either," said Orilin, "but now she is on to us."

"How can you tell?" asked Larilyn.

Orilin looked over to Orinda playing her harp.

"You told her you were from Acaida. She gathered that's where we might have met. And she knows that I'm an ex-Lorinthian Guardsman."

"How does she know that?" asked Larilyn. "Is that how she met you?"

"She got her start in Caltirion," he said. "It was when I was in the Guard. She's Hallintorian."

"But how do you know so much about her?"

Orilin looked puzzled.

"I know because she performed in Caltirion and brought many a man to their ruin."

Larilyn did not look convinced. In fact, she was angry. "Was she your lover?"

Orilin looked shocked.

"No," he said.

Larilyn shook her head and pushed aside the stew and the mead.

"I'm tired, Orilin," she said.

"Larilyn," he said. But she took her leave of him. She exited the tavern and went outside into the night.

Orilin just sat there confused. He really didn't know what to say. He had never touched Orinda, but he did not know how to convince Larilyn of that.

"Is your wife feeling okay, Orilin?" asked Gillen.

Orilin looked over at him.

"Orinda has gotten to her," he said.

Gillen smirked.

"She said something to offend her, I take it?"

"Orinda is just being herself," said Orilin. "I need to go look for Larilyn." Gillen nodded.

"You two should probably get some much needed

rest."

"I agree," said Orilin.

ᐱᐱᐱᐱᐱᐱ

Larilyn walked amongst a grove of pines a ways away from the town, trying to cope with her anger. Orinda was so rude. And Orilin knew way too much about her. She propped her head against a small cedar and sighed.

"Maybe I'm wrong," she whispered. "Maybe there is really nothing to this." She then shook her head. Her hands tightened.

"I hate her," she said with clenched teeth. Just then she heard footsteps behind her. She turned around.

"Orilin?" she said. But it was not him. There were three men. One drew a sword and the other two drew knives.

"Come here, lass," they said. Larilyn backed against the tree in fear.

"What do you want?!" she gasped. The man with a sword pointed it at her. She tried to run, but the two men with knives caught her by the throat with a cord. She felt it tighten around her mouth. She managed to get out one last cry.

"Orilin!" she cried loudly. And then the cord tightened and started to choke her. The men flung her to the ground and tied her wrists.

"You're not going anywhere, girl," breathed the one with the sword. He pressed the point of the sword against the back of her neck.

"Keep struggling with me or try anything, and I'll put this blade through your neck!" The other men laughed. One of them, plus the man with the sword picked her up and towed her away into the dark.

"She's beautiful," one said. "She will bring a good price."

Just then there was a flash of something. The third man turned around and was hit in the face with the blade of a sword. Blood and teeth were sent flying. The second man with the knife dropped his grip on Larilyn and rushed at their attacker. Orilin was there to meet him. The thug lunged at Orilin with his knife. Orilin blocked it with his sword and the knife shattered. Orilin then tripped him at the ankles and dropped him to the ground plunging his sword through the man's chest.

He wrenched his sword out of the dying man and rushed at the last thug who held Larilyn. But the man put his sword to Larilyn's throat.

"Take another step, Elf, and I will slit her from top to bottom!"

Orilin smiled at him.

"I've dealt with worse than you. Give her to me now and I won't give you a worse fate."

The man smiled but looked quite nervous. He pressed his sword harder against Larilyn's throat.

"You want to try me?!"

Orilin dropped his head and got down on his knee putting one hand in the dirt.

"Okay, okay," he said. "Just … where are you …"

"That's none of your concern, Elf," he said. Larilyn struggled. The man punched her in the stomach and she dropped, gagging. Orilin moved quickly. He took a handful of dirt, rose to his feet and threw the dirt into the thug's eyes.

"Agh!" the man yelled. Orilin swung his sword through the man's knee slashing through the tendons. He dropped, screaming. Orilin then swung his sword through the man's neck killing him with one blow.

He quickly went over to his wife and cut her bindings loose and the binding around her mouth.

"Orilin!" she screamed. She reached up and embraced him, fiercely crying into his shoulder.

"There, love," he whispered. "I've got you. I've got you. It's all over."

She sat sobbing into his shoulder as he looked up into the sky and sighed.

Chapter 8

ORILIN CONTINUED TO HOLD HIS WIFE AND LET her cry. She had never seen such horror, much less become part of it. He took her face in his hands.

"You're okay, love. You're okay. I'm here. Your little hawk is here."

She looked up at him, tears streaming from her eyes. She then kissed him.

"My little hawk," she whispered. Orilin just held her. They sat there for a while. She then looked up and held his face in her hands.

"I'm sorry, love. I should have not doubted you. I don't believe what I imagined about you and Orinda ..."

He touched one of her ears and looked into her eyes.

"Don't worry about a thing, love."

She laid her head back on his shoulder and he continued to hold her.

"What are we going to do, love?" she asked.

Orilin sighed.

"We need to get out of here."

Just then they heard the barking of dogs and the yelling of men. The guards came into the grove where the skirmish had taken place.

"Who are you?!" yelled one of the guards.

Orilin stood up.

"I'm Orilin Alandiron," he said. "And I had to protect my wife from these men."

The guards looked at each other.

"You are the famed warrior from Caltirion?" they asked. "What if we don't believe you?"

"He is Orilin Alandiron," said Larilyn wiping away some more tears. "My husband."

"Your word does not hold weight here, Elf woman," they said.

"Send us to Gillen at the Grey Fox," said Orilin. "He can vouch for us. Also, look at the slain. They are Menetarran slave-traders."

The guards went over to look at the dead men. One of them looked back at Orilin.

"Why do you say that?"

"I used to be a Lorinthian Guardsman. There are things going on in the world that you have no idea of."

The guard looked from him to Larilyn.

"You two will have to come with us. Give us your sword."

Orilin handed it to them.

"You will come with us to Gillen," they said. "We will see if he will vouch for you."

"Very well," said Orilin. "But I can also vouch for myself. Like I said, things in the world are quite dire right now. If you will hear me, I will speak to you of them."

"Later," said the guardsman. "To Gillen you go."

ᎶᎶᎶᎶᎶᎶ

People were leaving the Grey Fox for the night when the two Elves and the guardsmen arrived. The guards escorted them with spears, and the dogs followed. The people were alarmed at what they saw.

"What's going on here?" one asked.

One of the guards pushed him aside.

"Go on your way, you drunk!"

The man stumbled away. Orinda Hallison and Elandon walked out. Orinda saw some blood on Orilin's tunic.

"What have you done now, Orilin?" she asked shaking her head.

"That's none of your concern, Orinda!" he said firmly.

She smirked a little, shrugged, and went into the night. Elandon stopped for a bit.

"Are you two okay, Orilin?"

The Elf nodded.

"We're fine."

The guards led them into an empty tavern with the spears still pointing at them.

"Is it really necessary to make such a scene?" asked Orilin.

"We are calling the shots here, Elf," they said.

Orilin was getting more aggravated.

"Gillen!" he yelled. The plump man came out of the scullery and was appalled at what he saw.

"Orilin?! By the Creator, what has happened?"

"It's a long story."

Gillen approached them.

"Have you any idea who you have in custody?" he asked firmly. "This is Orilin Alandiron, former Lorinthian Guardsman and his wife, Larilyn."

The guards looked to each other.

"You are a trustworthy man, Gillen," they said. "Don't start to be otherwise now!"

"I'm not!" shouted Gillen. "Please put your spears down and let him speak."

The guards slowly lowered their spears and looked at each other. Their captain stepped up.

"Do you know that this Elf single-handedly slaughtered three armed men, Gillen?"

The innkeeper smirked.

"He has killed a lot more than that, I assure you!"

Larilyn's temper finally flared.

"This is crazy!" she said to the guards. "I am his wife! I was rescued by my husband from abduction."

The lead guard looked at her and stared.

"Loose their bonds but keep the Elf's sword," he said. The guards obeyed.

"This is stupid, Bodar," said Gillen.

"Quiet!" the lead guard firmly replied. He looked at Orilin.

"All right, Master Orilin, you may speak."

Orilin looked to Larilyn and then to the men.

"Who are you?" he asked.

"I'm Bodar," said the guard, "Captain of the guard here."

Orilin nodded.

"Orilin Alandiron."

Bodar smirked.

"Go on and tell us what is so dire."

Orilin looked to Larilyn again and then back to Bodar.

"We are traveling to Caltirion," he said.

"Does not sound so dire to me," said Bodar.

Gillen spoke up.

"They are indeed. They have a room in my inn."

Bodar looked to Orilin motioning him to continue. Orilin breathed deeply and pursed his lips.

"Like I said, we are traveling to Caltirion. Just a few days ago we were almost ambushed by a horde from the north accompanied by a Meldron leader. She looked as someone of great importance. My wife and I hid in the Dreath Wood hoping they would not follow us. They did not. But I heard some of the things of which they spoke. There are more Meldron scouts heading this way plus Menetarran hordes – right for Gallinthrar!"

There was a silence. The guards looked at each other.

"Ha, ha, ha!" they laughed.

"Laugh if you want," said Orilin. "I am telling the truth. Either way, I have committed no crime. I was defending my wife from abduction. Release me and let us continue to our destination."

Bodar shook his head rubbing his eyes.

"It's been a long night, Master Orilin," he said. "We will keep you in custody here until morning. That will give us more time to clear matters up."

"We cannot be delayed!" said Orilin. "We have to get to Caltirion."

Bodar shook his head.

"I have spoken. Tonight you will stay here."

$$\Upsilon \, \Upsilon \, \Upsilon \, \Upsilon \, \Upsilon \, \Upsilon$$

The two Elves were confined to their room the whole next day. They were let out only for meals, and neither got much sleep.

"I wonder how the Kesstals are doing?" asked Larilyn.

"I as well," Orilin said.

The night passed uneventful. The two were getting a little sleep when Captain Bodar burst through the door to their room with a little candle.

"There is something you need to see atop the watch-tower, Master Orilin." Orilin stood up and took Larilyn's hand.

"Lead on."

"Let us make haste," said Bodar.

The Captain led them out of the inn into the dark hours of the morning. He led them through a grove of pines and up a small rocky hill. Atop the hill was a very large stone tower with no roof. It had a fire signal a top it that was unlit. Captain Bodar lead them up the long steps up into the tower.

"What do you think is going on?" asked Larilyn to her husband.

"I don't think it's good," he remarked.

The three reached the top where two other guards were stationed. Both looked back at the three.

"Well, Captain Bodar?" asked Orilin.

The Captain pursed his lips and spoke.

"See for yourself."

Orilin looked out in the distance and began to see faint lights; many of them. Orilin knew they were not the lights of a town or city.

"O my Creator!" he said. Without hesitation he began to run down the steps of the tower and out across to the next rocky hill.

"Where's he going?" asked Bodar to Larilyn. She looked back at him.

"He's going to investigate."

"Investigate what?" continued Bodar.

"You should have believed him," she said. "Those are not the lights of a town!"

Orilin continued up the hill where the trees cleared into fields. He laid on the ground and put his ear to it. There was nothing; no sound. He looked back up again. The lights were still shining bright.

"O Creator," he prayed. "Spare us!"

He jumped to his feet and raced back to the watch-tower.

"Light the signal fire!" he shouted to Bodar. "Light it now!"

He ran back up the stairs to the top. Bodar was await-ing him.

"What are you waiting for?!" asked Orilin.

Bodar looked at him grimly.

"What is it?"

"What do you think it is?" said Orilin. "It's the Mene-tarran horde, and they are closer than I thought! They are a day out from Cedar Grove at best. All hamlets from Sargna up to here have been taken. We have friends in Sargna so light that …"

"It's the time for Pilgrimage for many," said Bodar. "How do I know it's not …"

"They are not Pilgrims!" said Orilin. "This will be the end of Cedar Grove if you do not light that fire. Signal for Gallinthrar! For them and for yourself!"

Bodar hesitated, but then spoke.

"I feared you would say as much. If it is the Menetarran horde riding to make war, then what about the Pilgrims?"

"Al-Nartha would be overrun. There are no more Pilgrimages right now! Barras Drin and a Meldron sorceress are riding south. This combined with the Menetarran horde could ..."

"Why?" asked Bodar. "Why would they ...?"

"Don't be a fool, Bodar," said Orilin. "Light the fire. War is upon us."

Bodar looked at Orilin fiercely.

"How do you two know so much?"

Orilin took a deep breath and sighed.

"Just a few days ago we ourselves were on Pilgrimage to Al-Nartha. We stopped in Acaida and lodged with our friend the Vicar Elimed. We were worshipping in Acaida's sanctuary when the bit of the Eternal Flame went out! We tried to ..."

"Went out?!" smirked Bodar. "The Eternal Flame does not go out!"

"It did," remarked Orilin. "Elimed told us to ride north to Caltirion to seek help from Hhrin-Calin and Lyrinias. Like I said, we hid in the Dreath Wood where we were almost overtaken by Barras Drin and the Meldron woman. We took the ferry into Hallintor and here we are. If you don't want to believe me that is your problem. All I want you to do is light that fire!"

"Lighting a signal fire for Gallinthrar troops is my problem indeed, Master Orilin," remarked Bodar. "That is if there is nothing to this."

"There is something to this, Bodar!" said Larilyn. "My husband is telling the truth. Light the fire!"

There was a long silence between them all.

"Why did you call us up here, Bodar?" asked Orilin. "You didn't call us up here just to see the pretty night sky."

Bodar shook his head.

"No indeed."

"Don't you believe us?" asked Larilyn. "Don't you believe we are who we say we are?"

Bodar paced and looked back at them.

"To tell you the truth, we are afraid. What if you are right?"

Orilin shook his head.

"If I am wrong you can have me flogged yourself," said Orilin.

"Orilin!" said Larilyn.

Bodar stepped up to him.

"Lighting a signal fire for no reason, Master Orilin, is punishable by death. If we light this fire and these are only lights of travelling pilgrims; then you will be hanged and your wife will become a widow. Do you have children?"

"No," said Orilin.

"Then all the worse fate for your wife, Master Orilin. Besides, I myself don't particularly want to be hanged with you, nor do any of my men."

There was another long silence. Orilin and Larilyn looked to each other. Orilin held her shoulders.

"You said you trusted me."

She nodded and squeezed his hands. He swallowed hard and his voice went hoarse.

"You know that I love you," he said. "I do this for us, for the Kesstals and for all of Telbyrin."

She embraced him tightly.

"I know, love," she said.

He slowly let go.

"All right, Captain Bodar," said Orilin. "Let me light the fire. Let me do it and I will be the only one to blame if there is any wrong."

"It's not that easy, Master Orilin," remarked Bodar. "My men and I must allow you to light the fire. In that, we share in the responsibility."

Orilin nodded. He then punched Bodar in the side of the head knocking him out with one blow. The other guards responded with their spears. One thrust for Orilin's chest, but the Elf stepped aside and caught it, kicked the man in the sciatic nerve and with the other motion hammered the other guard in the head with the shaft. Orilin quickly knocked him out. The man kicked in the sciatic nerve rolled in pain on the ground.

Larilyn was stunned.

"Get the flint and steel from his belt quickly, love," said Orilin. The man kicked in the leg reached for his dagger but Orilin kicked it out of the way. He then brought the end of the shaft of the spear to the man's head and knocked him out.

"No responsibility now, Captain Bodar," said Orilin.

Larilyn reached into Bodar's belt and brought out flint and steel.

"Some negotiating," she said.

Orilin smirked back. He took the flint and steel to an unlit torch of pitch and lit it. He then tossed it into the signal fire.

"We have to get out of here!" he said to his wife.

"Agreed," said Larilyn. Orilin grabbed his sword from Captain Bodar and they made their way down the tower quickly.

"How do we get out of here?" asked Larilyn.

"We go upstream. We have to keep going until we reach Gallinthrar."

He took her hand, and they started running.

"They will send dogs once they have discovered Bodar," said Orilin. "We have to move as fast as we can." Larilyn nodded. The two Elves, with nothing but a sword and the clothes on their back, dashed off into the remaining night.

Chapter 9

THE ELVES RAN UPSTREAM AS FAST AS THEY could, weaving and moving through briers and thickets. Orilin chopped some out of the way with his sword.

"They are going to find us with all the mess we are making," said Larilyn.

"That can't be helped now," said Orilin. "We have to keep moving or we die."

They were both thinking how fortunate it was that the moon was out. The moonlight glowed off the stream so they could see their way.

"We should have brought a light," said Larilyn. "The moonlight might fail." Orilin chopped some more hedges out of the way.

"We have to work with what we have."

Orilin sheathed his sword and led his wife across some river rocks and they crossed the small river; the rapids gushing past them. Larilyn slipped on one of the rocks and she fell knee deep in the water. Orilin quickly caught her before the rapids could take her away.

"Agh!" she spat. Orilin pulled her out of the water

and sat her up on the rocks again.

"Sorry," she said.

Orilin smiled a bit.

"No worries. Let's go."

They soon ran out of the thickets and went up a large hill. A large buck ran past them out of the shrubs and spooked Orilin. He unsheathed his sword and backed up. Larilyn stayed his arm.

"Just a deer, love," she said. "Let's hurry."

There was a large grassy hill up ahead with some small, smooth rocks.

The two climbed the hill, which opened up into a large view of the Gallinthrar fields.

"I hope the Creator is with us," said Orilin. "Otherwise we are dead."

Larilyn took his hand and led them as they ran.

"Stop thinking like that," she said. "We have to make it." The two ran on ahead.

"Do you think the city has seen the fire yet?" asked Larilyn.

Orilin looked at her.

"Yes. I hope they are sending out scouts as we speak." More smooth rocks were in the field among some sharp ones.

"Watch these rocks," said Orilin.

The two ran on. Both were getting tired. Sweat ran down their faces and backs. Something sharp was under Larilyn's foot. She dodged it and stepped up on a smooth rock. It was slippery. She slipped and fell while catching another sharp rock. It twisted her ankle. She cried and went down. Orilin ran back to her. She was holding her ankle and crying out.

"It's sprained," he said.

"Agh! You think?!" shouted Larilyn. She lay her head back on the ground in pain. Orilin looked back toward Cedar Grove. He saw nothing as of yet.

"I don't see anything," he said to his wife. "But it won't be long until we do. We have to move."

Larilyn scoffed.

"I can't move like this!" she yelled. "I guess we will just have to die!"

Orilin looked up and then back at her.

"I told you to watch the rocks."

Larilyn gritted her teeth.

"Well…just leave me!"

"No!" yelled Orilin.

Larilyn glared at him.

"If you had not beaten all those men senseless we would not be in this mess! How could you have been so stupid?!"

He glared back at her.

"If I didn't we would have never gotten that fire lit."

"We could have just left Cedar Grove in peace and…"

"I guess you forgot we were being held prisoner, Larilyn!"

She went silent for a moment. Orilin looked around and spied a large rock jutting out from the ground. It was about three feet in height.

"We will have to hide," he said. "Behind that rock right there."

Larilyn looked to it and tried to get up.

"Let me help you," he said.

"No," she said. "Just get away."

She tried, but could not stand on her ankle. She crawled on the ground toward the rocks.

"Larilyn!" yelled Orilin.

She did not respond. He calmed himself and went over to her.

"Listen," he said. "I know you are angry with me right now. In one sense I don't blame you. But I cannot leave you here just to crawl on your belly." Then he heard it. A small rumbling. He put his ear to the ground and then looked up. There were lights in the distance.

"They are coming, Larilyn," he said.

She glared at him.

"This is all your fault," she seethed.

He was hurt by her words, but he looked up and saw the mob still on their way.

"Larilyn," he said.

She looked at him.

"Let me carry you to that rock." She glared at him again and propped her arm around his neck. He carried her to the high rock and lay her gently behind it. He then looked up again. The lights were getting brighter. Just then there were two other lights; lights from the forest up north. They were getting closer. Orilin could also make out the first streaks of dawn as well. He didn't know what to do.

"What are those lights right there?" he asked.

"How should I know?" said Larilyn.

He looked at it again.

"That's one of the men from Gallinthrar."

Orilin hid behind the rock with his wife.

"Will you forgive me, love?" he asked.

Larilyn closed her eyes.

"Orilin …"

Just then there were voices. Orilin unsheathed his sword.

"What do you think you're doing?" asked Larilyn.

He looked at her and smirked.

"If they reach us before those riders from the north do, I'll have to take matters into my own hands again."

Larilyn closed her eyes and held her ankle.

"Great," she sighed. The rumbling of the horses got closer and they were almost upon them. Dogs could be heard as well.

"Orilin ..." said Larilyn. But they were upon them.

"Find them!" yelled one man. "They are close." Orilin knew it was futile at this time. He slowly dropped his sword. It would be futile to try to fight them. He would be killed quickly. There were too many of them and they had bows. He got up, dropped his sword and held up his hands.

"Orilin!" gasped Larilyn. But he continued to walk towards them.

"Men of Cedar Grove!" he shouted. "I surrender my sword ..." But he was struck with an arrow up in the left shoulder. It knocked him back and he fell to the ground; his head striking a rock.

"Orilin!" screamed Larilyn. "Orilin! My little hawk! Orilin!"

The man who had shot him dismounted. Larilyn crawled over to her husband.

"Orilin!" she cried; tears streaming down her cheeks as she held him. He looked up at her.

"I'm sorry, love," he groaned. She shook her head.

"It's going to be okay, love," she cried. "I'm here."

He looked up at her, touched her face and blacked out. She embraced him.

"Orilin!" she wept. "Orilin!" She shook him, but he did not respond.

"Orilin!" The man who had shot him came up to her and unsheathed his sword. Larilyn, in hot anger, grabbed her husband's sword and stood up.

"Get away from him!" she growled. The man with the sword smiled.

"Put that thing down, miss, or I'll end you very quickly."

Just then the riders from the north arrived. They were clad in silver armor and red cloaks. One of them took off his plumed helmet and dismounted.

"What is going on here?" he demanded. The man who had threatened Larilyn spoke up.

"These Elves assaulted three men on our watchtower in Cedar Grove. Furthermore, they even lit the signal fire. If this is some sort of Elven prank, Cedar Grove won't stand for it. Lighting the signal fire for no reason is punishable by ..."

"I know very well, constable, thank you!" shouted the armored man. He looked down to the Elf who lay on the ground; the arrow protruding from his left shoulder.

"Orilin Alandiron!" he gasped. "Ride on, constable. I will take it from here." The constable shook his head.

"He is in our custody. He will be tried and hanged."

"No, he will not!" said the armored man. "I am Hadar of Gallinthrar; Captain of the First Rank. This Elf was a Lorinthian Guard. I know him. He is a friend. Furthermore, King Lyrinias and Vicar Elrad want him and that certainly trumps your orders. And I am sure he did not light that signal fire for a prank! I will take him to them."

"If you interfere ..." said the constable.

"If you strike me down," said Hadar, "Gallinthrar will come and burn your miserable town. Think twice on what you do, constable. Consider it very well. Orilin Alandiron will come with me."

The constable sheathed his sword; his pride clearly hurt.

"Very well," he said. "But if he ever steps foot in

Cedar Grove again …"

"Yes, constable. Ride out!"

The constable gritted his teeth and stepped up into his saddle.

"Ride out!" he shouted.

The mob from Cedar Grove rode back from whence they came behind the rising sun. Hadar looked down at Larilyn holding her husband. He bent down.

"Who are you, my lady?"

She looked up.

"I am Larilyn Alandiron. Orilin's wife." He took a knee and bowed to her.

"It is an honor," he said. "Your husband is a great hero. Not only of Caltirion and Hallintor but of all Telbyrin. It would be my honor to escort you with your husband to Gallinthrar's gates." Larilyn looked back down to her husband.

"Most of all he was my hero," she sobbed. "He was my soul-mate. He was my …"

"He is not dead, my lady," said Hadar. "Here. Feel his life blood." He put her fingers on his neck and she could feel a pulse.

"We have to get him to Gallinthrar soon if he is going to live, though," said Hadar. "Shall we ride?"

"Yes!" said Larilyn immediately. "With utmost haste! Otherwise I am bound to Fade!"

Chapter 10

Hadar took Larilyn on his horse and his assistant, Torla, took Orilin.

"Will he survive?" asked Larilyn anxiously.

"I believe so," said Hadar. "Lorinthian Guard fight to the last breath. He is losing blood though. We will have to cauterize the wound once we remove the arrow. It will take him some time to recover."

"Cauterize the wound?!' exclaimed Larilyn. "That will nearly kill him!" Hadar looked back at her and shook his head.

"I doubt it. It will take much more than that to kill Orilin. Besides, he is hanging on for you."

Larilyn looked back to Torla carrying her husband. She nodded.

"Twice he has saved me on this trip," said Larilyn.

Hadar looked back to her again.

"We recently received word of Lyrinias and Elrad looking for your husband. If you don't mind my asking, my lady, how is it that they seek for him so badly? There is rumor that something untoward is happening in the world. Is that the reason?"

"Yes," said Larilyn.

Hadar's eyes narrowed.

"What is it, if I may ask?"

Larilyn sighed and looked at him.

"A few days ago we went to Acaida with the family we live nearby. We worshiped there at the Sanctuary when we experienced a terrible event. The bit of the Eternal Flame went out in Acaida. The Vicar Elimed bid us ride for Caltirion with utmost haste. We made our way through the Dreath Wood, bypassing a horde of barbarians from the North led by a Meldron sorceress. They talked of Menetarran hordes coming to Gallinthrar. We met a Vicar named Raltaron speaking of Caltirion needing my husband. He did not lead us but told us that our ways must be separate. We made our way to Cedar Grove. There we met with much trouble. There were Menetarran slave traders in the town. Orilin saved me from three of them and killed them. We were taken into custody by the constables and held up in a local inn. They summoned us the next night to the watchtower where we saw many lights in the south. The constables thought they might be lights from the pilgrims to Al-Nar-tha, but my husband knew better. They were the lights of the Menetarran horde. Orilin, after disabling the con-stables because of their stubbornness, took me and fled up to this point. So you find us now. I know this is hard to believe but …"

"Not really," said Hadar. "Our scouts have al-ready reported sightings of Barras Drin's horde. I thought it was simply a stirring in the North that we would have to deal with. Since you have seen them already however, there seems to be more to the sto-ry. You and your husband cannot stay in Gallinthrar for long. I have to get you to Caltirion. You will be safer there. We will heal Orilin in Gallinthrar and then move on. As for the Flame going out, I can only pray to the Creator that He is still with us."

Larilyn nodded.

The four soon arrived at the massive gates of the city of Gallinthrar. It was fully dawn by now.

"Ho! Open for Captain Hadar!' yelled one of the guards. The gates opened up and the four rode in. They were met by many people. Some gasped knowing who Orilin was.

"Orilin Alandiron!"

"Let us through!" said Captain Hadar.

The people continued talking.

"Is he dead?"

"No!" shouted Hadar. "Let us through."

A Human Vicar strode up to Hadar and Torla.

"Bring him to the Vicarage, Hadar," he said. "There I will heal him."

"Thank you, Lau," said the Captain. The Vicar Lau made his way through the crowds telling them to pass. The Vicarage was just up ahead. It was a dark brown wooded building with a pointed roof. The Sanctuary was attached.

"Bring him in quickly!" said Lau. Hadar and Larilyn dismounted and she hobbled over to Orilin. Torla helped him down. Torla followed Lau carrying Orilin into the Vicarage while Hadar shut the door behind them and locked it.

Lau carried them into a room where he treated many for illnesses. Besides being a Vicar, he was also Gallinthrar's primary physician.

"We could not be in a better place for this," remarked Larilyn to Lau.

The Vicar shook his head.

"Hardly. Caltirion could treat him much better.

Who are you, if I may ask, my lady?"

"I'm Larilyn Alandiron, his wife."

Lau bowed his head.

"'Tis an honor."

Larilyn smiled a bit. Lau placed Orilin on the bed and examined the wound.

"I'll help in whatever way I can," said Hadar. Lau moved his long, brown hair out of the way and looked back at the Captain.

"Go get a hot iron from a forge, Captain. Hurry!"

Hadar left hastily and warned Torla to watch the door. Lau continued his work. He put a flask of water in Larilyn's hands.

"Give him this water. We have to hydrate him."

"He is so pale!" said Larilyn. Lau nodded.

"He is losing blood. Give him the water. He is slipping in and out of consciousness but he should drink it. Hurry." Larilyn nodded and put the flask to her husband's lips. He groaned and greedily drank from the flask until it was half-consumed. Meanwhile Lau boiled water and put strong smelling herbs in it.

Hadar knocked and Torla let him in. In his hand was a red-hot iron.

"Watch out!" he said making his way through. Lau looked up at him.

"Give him some more water, Lady Larilyn," he said. "Hadar, give the iron to Torla and help me get this arrow out. You will have to hold him." Hadar nodded and did as the Vicar ordered. They held Orilin down on the bed as Lau grabbed a pair of shears from a box of medical instruments. He went behind Orilin's shoulder and snapped the tip of the arrow off. Orilin winced in pain. Larilyn gave him more water.

"Orilin!" said Lau in the Elf's ear. "This is Lau! Larilyn is here with me. So is your friend Hadar. We are going to save you now. You are going to live to see better days."

He swallowed and sighed.

"Orilin. This next procedure is going to hurt. I'm going to give you some ether now."

Lau grabbed a rag and poured a bit of ether on it. He pressed it to Orilin's nose and the Elf breathed deep. His head dropped a little.

"This will numb the pain a bit," Lau said to Larilyn. "Now we have to act very quickly or he will die."

He looked to Torla.

"Torla, hand the iron to Hadar. Hadar, on my mark, cauterize the wound. I'm going to free the arrow from him now. On my mark!"

Hadar nodded. Lau sighed.

"This is going to hurt."

Larilyn held Orilin as best she could. Lau, with one quick motion, freed the arrow from Orilin's shoulder. Blood spurted and he cried out.

"Now, Hadar!" shouted Lau. Hadar plunged the hot iron into Orilin's shoulder. He screamed out.

"Flip him over!" yelled Lau. "Quickly!" Torla helped Larilyn flip him. Hadar plunged the iron into Orilin's back wound. He screamed again and passed out.

"Hold him!" shouted Lau. The Vicar quickly poured the hot water that smelled strongly of the herbs into the wound. He poured it graciously on the front and back.

"This is a coagulant," said the Vicar nervously. "This should help continue to stop the bleeding. Keep giving him water, Lady Larilyn."

She pressed the water flask to Orilin's lips but he would not drink. He was totally unconscious. Lau felt of a pulse on the neck.

"Does he live?" asked Hadar.

"Yes," said Lau. "But he may not live long."

"What do you mean?" demanded Larilyn.

Lau sighed and looked at her.

"He may die, my lady."

Larilyn looked at him in anger.

"No!" she shouted.

"There is nothing more I can do," said Lau. "All we can do now is pray."

Larilyn shook her head.

"Get the Flame!" she shouted.

Lau's eyes widened.

"Get the Flame!" shouted Larilyn. "Is it still lit?"

"Yes," said Lau.

"Then get it!" shouted Larilyn again. "You are a Vicar. You know that the Flame can heal!"

"It can also destroy!" said Lau strongly.

Larilyn shook her head.

"It won't. He is a hero. He is a hero of Telbyrin!"

The four sat in silence for a moment.

"What are we waiting for?!" yelled Larilyn.

Lau glared at her.

"You better be right about this, my lady. My head will be on a platter if you are not!"

"Let the blame fall on me!" said Larilyn.

Lau gritted his teeth and made his way to the Sanctuary. Larilyn continued to hold her husband, crying and singing into his ear.

"Hold on, love!" she said. "Hold on. I love you. I love you, my little hawk."

Lau reappeared with the bright Flame in his hands. Hadar and Torla reverently backed away. The Vicar knelt beside Larilyn.

"Let us pray." He led them in a quick but reverent prayer to the Creator that He might look upon Orilin and them with mercy. When the prayer was concluded he looked to Larilyn.

"Are you ready?"

Larilyn nodded.

Lau gently placed the Flame into Orilin's wound. It gently but wildly enveloped it. The gust of the Flame blew Larilyn's hair back a bit as she held Orilin's arm. Orilin groaned. Larilyn saw it as tears streamed down her face. The wound was sealing up. Lau smiled. He continued to hold the Flame to Orilin.

"It is working!" he said.

Orilin groaned again. The wound was virtually gone by now. Lau then gently took the Flame away. They all said a prayer of thanksgiving to the Creator. They sat in silence for a while. Larilyn closed her eyes and continued to weep a little. Lau eventually broke the silence.

"I must take the Flame back to the Sanctuary." He turned around to do so and it was then that the Flame gently went out. Lau stared in horror at what he saw.

"Has this happened where you have come from, my lady?!" he asked Larilyn.

"Yes," she said. "It happened in Acaida. Evidently it has happened in Caltirion also."

"It has," added Captain Hadar.

Lau looked at both of them.

"We met a Vicar named Raltaron in the Dreath Wood who had a piece of the Flame," Larilyn continued.

"Raltaron, you say?" asked Lau.

"Yes," replied Larilyn.

Lau sighed and looked down and his now empty hands.

"He has come then from the Airell Mountains where the Enclave is. I hope he has an answer for us."

Larilyn narrowed her gaze.

"Who is Raltaron?"

Lau looked at her in bewilderment.

"He is the Vicar of the Airell Enclave; one of the most renown Vicars in Telbyrin."

Larilyn looked at him in wonder.

"Then it is true. There is a large Enclave of Elves in the Airell Mountains!"

Lau nodded.

"Yes. Your people are not just a scattered people throughout Telbyrin. This Enclave is growing strong."

Larilyn looked back to her husband, embraced him and looked up to Lau again.

"I wish we could take him there," she said.

Lau nodded and sighed.

"I do as well. But Lyrinias apparently needs him."

Larylin stared back at them.

"He cannot serve the king like this. Let him out of this, I beg you. We have done our part. We have brought the news of the Flame to you. What more can we do?"

Lau stared at her.

"I don't know. But we have to get you to Caltirion for two reasons. One is that the king requests your husband. The other is that war is upon our gates. Gallinthrar is a small city-state. You will be much safer in Caltirion."

"He is right, my lady," said Hadar.

Larilyn shook her head.

"You don't have to call me that. I'm only a farm girl."

"You are the wife of a Lorinthian Guard and a hero of Caltirion," said Lau. "That hardly makes you just a common farm girl."

Larilyn looked down at her husband and then back up at Hadar.

"Can you get us there as quickly as possible, Captain Hadar?" The Captain nodded.

"On my honor, I will get you there by tomorrow."

Chapter 11

LARILYN HAD NEVER SEEN ANYTHING LIKE IT. THE Great City of Hallintor. Caltirion the Great. Over its battlements and main gates was a huge stature of Alrihon, the First King of Caltirion. The guards knew Captain Hadar and Torla and they let the party through. Larilyn beheld the stone walls lined with soldiers and guards of unique precision. They entered the city itself, its people scattered through the streets going on about their daily life as best as possible. There were Humans and Elves alike. There were horses and carts going throughout the streets. She saw the shops lining the streets of every sort. People were busy with their daily tasks, but Larilyn could tell that they were nervous about something. Military went through the streets by dozens in neat rows.

Up ahead, Larilyn saw the great palace of Caltirion. She looked up and then back to Captain Hadar.

"Is that the palace of the king?" she asked.

Hadar nodded.

"It is. And that is where I am taking you immediately."

Larilyn sighed. This was a long way off from a common farm in Sargna. This was a whole new world.

They were carrying Orilin in a cart with a top, pulled by a packhorse. He was sound asleep and had not fully awoken since he was rendered unconscious from the cauterization. Torla was at the front of the cart keeping watch over him. Hadar wanted to keep their cargo secret.

They kept making their way up to the palace gates. A man, a butcher by the looks of him, came strolling up to Hadar's horse.

"Any news from Gallinthrar, Captain? What about the Flame?"

"All continues at its best, Goodman," he responded. The butcher knew they were in a hurry and scurried out of the way.

Next, two Elven males in silver armor and plumed helmets ran up to them. They were holding spears and circular shields were slung on their backs.

"Who are these soldiers?" asked Larilyn. Hadar looked back at her.

"They are Lorinthian Guard," he said. "Let me do the speaking." The Elves came up and saluted Hadar. Hadar saluted back.

"What news from the south, Captain?" asked one. Hadar bowed his head.

"A Menetarran horde advances toward Gallinthrar. I and my assistant have this Elf woman and the Little Hawk." The Elven warrior nodded.

"We will escort you to the king's palace." They led them through another small crowd and past a fountain. There was another statue of Alrihon there.

"Fly open the gates!" yelled the warrior. The gates soon opened. Larilyn's eyes widened. The castle was immense and she didn't know how anyone could possibly get to the king. The walls were thick and heavily guarded on every station by Lorinthian Guard.

More of the Guard strolled out in double file and snapped to attention. Then there came a Human warrior of immense stature. He took off his plumed helmet, and his hair was all but shaved off. He came up to Hadar.

"Captain Hadar," he said.

Hadar leaped off his horse and bowed.

"Captain Aldanar," he responded.

Hadar took attention.

"Captain. I have arrived with Orilin Alandiron." Aldanar bowed.

"Is he safe?" Hadar nodded.

"He is. This is his wife, Larilyn." Aldanar bowed to her.

"'Tis a pleasure, my lady," he said. "I am Aldanar, Captain of the Lorinthian Guard. I am at your service."

"Thank you, sir," said Larilyn. She was not used to these formalities. Aldanar bowed again and turned to meet a couple walking forth. There was a man clad in a long, golden robe accompanied by a woman with long, golden hair dressed in a silver gown with a silver belt.

"Hail Lyrinias!" yelled Aldanar.

"Hail!" shouted the Guard all together as they snapped to attention.

"Off the horse!" whispered Hadar to Larilyn. She dismounted quickly and bowed. King Lyrinias was of average build. He had black curly hair, shortly cropped, and a black neatly trimmed beard. He looked to be in his early thirties. His queen was a woman of beauty. She had a bit of a pale complexion with green eyes.

King Lyrinias and his queen came up to the cart pulled by the packhorse.

"Has something happened?" asked King Lyrinias.

Hadar swallowed hard and looked up.

"Yes, my liege."

"May I see him?" asked the king.

"Of course, my liege," answered Hadar. He opened the top of the cart for the king, and in lay Orilin still fast asleep. Lyrinias and his queen peered in, and they stood in silence for some time.

"He is dirty," said Lyrinias, "but looks healthy nonetheless. You must have traveled in haste, Captain Hadar."

"Yes, my lord," he said. "We came as fast as we could." Lyrinias looked with pity on Orilin. He pulled back the sleeve of Orilin's tunic which revealed the scar from the arrow.

"Yet it looks as if this wound had never been. Who treated him, Captain?"

"Lau of Gallinthrar, my liege."

Lyrinias smiled a bit.

"He is a master physician then."

"He used the Flame on him, my lord," continued Hadar. With that Lyrinias' countenance went serious. He nodded and looked to Larilyn.

"Who are you, my lady?" asked Lyrinias.

"I am Larilyn Alandiron, sire," she said meekly. "I am his wife."

Lyrinias stared at her. He took her hand and kissed it.

"You are most welcome in Caltirion," he responded. "This is my wife and queen, Lirana." The tall queen bowed her head to Larilyn.

"It's a pleasure, my lady," said Larilyn.

"As is mine indeed," responded Lirana. "Come in. We will get you both cleaned and well fed. You look exhausted Lady Larilyn. And you look hurt yourself."

"I am," she said. "But I am most worried about my husband. I hope he wakes from his sleep."

Lirana smiled at her.

"The Flame has taken great care of him. Come now."

The king and queen led them through the iron gates to the palace, and the Guard followed them back in double file. Hadar and Torla stopped at the entrance.

"This is where we must part, my lady," said Hadar to Larilyn.

Larilyn stared at them.

"I never thanked you for saving our lives," she said.

"It was my honor," said Hadar. Larilyn quickly embraced him and Torla.

"The Creator bless you both," she said to them.

"It was our pleasure, my lady," responded Torla.

She looked back at them.

"I cannot repay you enough. Please tell Vicar Lau the same. I never got a chance to really thank him."

"I will," said Hadar. "Pray for Gallinthrar, though. We have to defend the south from the Menetarran horde now. War is upon us."

Lyrinias looked back.

"Caltirion will send aid," he said. "It is as I have feared and as Raltaron had told me. I will send aid under the command of two dozen of the Guard." Hadar bowed and saluted.

"We are most gracious, my liege." Lyrinias nodded.

"Come," he said to his wife. "Let us get our dear friend in and clean him."

The gates were shut and Hadar and Torla rode away.

ᛉ ᛉ ᛉ ᛉ ᛉ ᛉ

It was a beautiful night; as much as could be expected before the dawn of war. The stars shone bright and the moon was a waning gibbous now. It was the night after they had met the king and queen. Larilyn had slept for hours after their long journey with a medicinal wrap around her hurt ankle. She was amazed to feel how quickly and how much it helped. She was not happy that she was separated from Orilin but she knew that they needed to clean him up. She was left to a quiet bedchamber illumined only by the moonlight. Larilyn had just finished taking a bath and sat relaxing in a long robe on a recliner. An Elven maid, rather young-looking, came into the chamber with some new clothes.

"May I come in, my lady?" she asked.

Larilyn looked up and smirked just a little.

"I have never been called that in all my 300 years."

The maid smiled.

"That is who you are. You are Master Orilin's wife."

Larilyn smiled and sat up.

"Yes, please come in. What's your name?

"I am Iomil, my lady."

Larilyn looked at her.

"You don't have to call me that, Iomil. Please, just between you and me, call me Larilyn."

Iomil smiled.

"Yes, my la … ah … Larilyn." She walked over to her and put down the new clothes.

"What are these?!" exclaimed Larilyn. "They are beautiful."

"It is a Caltirion gown for ladies. May I tend to you, Larilyn?"

"What do you mean?"

"Well," said Iomil. "You need new yarn in your hair. You like to wear yarn, don't you? I will pull the tangles out of your hair, give you new yarn and a perfume. I will also put a fresh wrap on your ankle."

Larilyn smiled.

"Sounds lovely."

Iomil nodded and went to work. She hummed a song while she worked on Larilyn's hair.

Larilyn looked back at her.

"Have you lived in Caltirion all your life?"

"All my life," Iomil responded.

"How did you come to be in the king's service."

"I am skilled in healing as well as cosmetics," she said. "I want to be a physician more than anything. The king liked the idea of me having both skills and he employed me in his service."

"I have never dreamed of this life," said Larilyn. "My husband has talked about it with me, but experiencing it first-hand is really something."

"Yes," said Iomil. She had de-tangled Larilyn's hair and was now starting to put small twists of Elven yarn in small locks.

"Are you married, Iomil?" asked Larilyn.

The Elf maid blushed a little.

"No," she said. "But I have my eye on someone."

Larilyn looked back to her and smiled.

"Who?"

Iomil sighed.

"He is 175 years old and he is a wonderful musician. He serves in the army here too."

"Is he part of the Lorinthian Guard?" asked Larilyn.

"No," she answered. "But he is something! He sings to me every time he gets a chance. He plays the harp."

"As does my husband," said Larilyn.

Iomil nodded.

"Yes. When your husband was here, he would play in the king's hall. All would listen to him."

Larilyn grinned.

"I love it when he plays to me. Iomil, I hope you find your true soul-mate."

She smiled.

ᚺᚺᚺᚺᚺᚺ

It was past midnight. Larilyn could not sleep. Iomil had long since left, and she was alone on the balcony, clothed in her new gown. She looked out into the distance of Caltirion and to the fields of Hallintor. Way in the distance she could see lights. She did not know if they were lights from Gallinthrar or of the dreaded hordes. No signs of war could she see, and that was a relief. Perhaps things would not be as bad as everyone had planned. She hoped that, but it was only a thin hope. Most of all, she thought about Orilin.

Larilyn heard footsteps behind her.

"I'm okay, Iomil," she said. "I'll go to sleep soon. You need your rest too."

"That's about the most gorgeous farm girl I have ever seen," said a familiar voice.

Larilyn quickly turned around. It was Orilin clad in a simple white tunic, barefoot and with dark trousers.

"My love," she gasped. She embraced Orilin in a fierce kiss.

"I thought you were going to die!" she continued. "We tried everything. We even used the Flame on you! Orilin, I'm so sorry … I …"

"Larilyn," he whispered as he held her. "I'm here."

"I'm sorry, love," she sighed.

"For what?" he asked.

She looked up to him.

"For treating you so badly. For not being grateful for what you did for me back on the plains."

"That's behind us now, love," he said. "You are well, as am I. And I can use my arm fine. The Flame worked. And it took courage for you to use it. Did it go out?"

"Yes," said Larilyn. "And things are getting worse."

Orilin took her by the shoulders and looked in her eyes.

"Not where I'm standing."

She smiled and embraced him.

$$\Upsilon \; \Upsilon \; \Upsilon \; \Upsilon \; \Upsilon \; \Upsilon$$

The next morning, Orilin and Larilyn were summoned to the royal throne room of King Lyrinias and Queen Lirana. Orilin was given a Caltirion robe made up of gold, silver and crimson. New sandals were put on his feet. It was quite a change from the boots, tunic and the trousers of Sargna. Larilyn went in at his side and they both bowed to the throne. King Lyrinias dismounted and pointed his scepter to them. Then he came down and embraced Orilin.

"My old friend," he said.

Orilin smiled.

"Lyrinias."

The king held his shoulders and continued to smile.

"It is so good to see you. To see you and see you well." A familiar figure came forth from the crowd of dignitaries around the throne. He was an Elf of immense height and had brown hair and silver eyes. He was clad in a gold and silver robe.

"Orilin," he said softly.

Orilin looked up.

"Elrad!" he exclaimed. He went up and embraced the Vicar with tears welling up in his eyes.

"Yes," said Elrad. "How good to have you home."

Elrad looked to Larilyn.

"And your beautiful wife. How blessed you are."

Larilyn smiled. Orilin looked back to Larilyn and then to Elrad.

"I have so much to tell you, father."

Elrad nodded.

"I will have plenty of time, son."

Another familiar figure came up. He was another Elf with brown hair and eyes.

"Master Martralin," said Orilin. "It is so great to see you."

Martralin smiled and took Orilin's shoulders.

"And you, Orilin. Welcome home."

Orilin looked around with playful glee.

"This is so wonderful," he said. "I am truly honored."

Lyrinias smiled.

"We will have a feast in your honor tonight. But, unfortunately, there are pressing matters to attend to as you know. War is upon our gates, Orilin."

Orilin nodded grimly.

"I know. There is so much I have to tell you."

Lyrinias nodded and looked back.

"Everyone!" he said in a loud voice. "The Arch Vicar of Telbyrin: Hhrin-Calin!"

A tall man strode forth with white hair speckled with black, a gold and brown robe and a white beard. Orilin and everyone else bowed deeply. The man walked up to Orilin carrying a staff with an eagle's claw on it on which to place the Flame.

"Your Reverence," said Orilin. "It is always an honor."

Hhrin-Calin bowed his head slightly.

"We know of the Flame, Orilin," he said. "And we sent messengers to Gallinthrar and to the Airell Enclave in search for you. Elrad rode with haste to the Enclave thinking that you might be among the Airell Elves."

Orilin pursed his lips and looked up at the Arch-Vicar.

"I have been living in Sargna since I left the Guard, your Reverence."

The crowd looked confused.

"Why Sargna?" asked Martralin.

Lyrinias looked to him.

"Please, Master Martralin. This is not the time to question Orilin about his choices for a home. Please continue, your Reverence."

Hhrin-Calin nodded and continued.

"It is a blessing and an answer to prayers that you are here, Orilin."

Orilin shook his head.

"Why me, your Reverence? Why am I needed here?"

Hhrin-Calin looked to King Lyrinias.

"Because Elrad and I wanted you to fight on our side," he said. "We wanted the best swordsman in Caltirion in our army again. When the Flame went out and we almost immediately started hearing of armies from the North, we wanted you back." Orilin looked up to his friend.

"What difference can one Elf make in your army, my liege, even though you hold this Elf in high-esteem?"

Lyrinias nodded.

"We held counsel last night, Orilin. There is a Menetarran horde coming from the south as you know. There is Barras Drin coming from the north, and the Meldron are apparently involved. And now the Flame is going out. The hearts of our warriors are shaken, even among the Guard. What confidence can they have watching the Flame disappearing? What confidence can they have in these times without the Little Hawk?"

"As I have heard before, my brother," said Orilin. "The Flame is not the Creator. Let them have faith in the Creator."

"The Flame is the visible symbol of hope," continued Lyrinias. "Orilin, we need you. I know you don't want to get involved or go back into war but we need you to give morale back our men. When you would stride out in the past with the Guard, the enemy was badly shaken. They fear you, and our men respect you utmost. You are the fierce Little Hawk." Orilin looked up.

"What about my wife?"

"She will be protected behind these walls. You have

my word that she will be."

Orilin started to pace a little.

"We have friends in Sargna, my liege. Right now they are in danger. What about them?"

"You will help them most by focusing the brunt of the attack on the Menetarran horde, warding them away from concentration on Sargna," said Lyrinias. "Gallinthrar has already pledged to fight them. Indeed, they have no choice."

Lyrinias paused.

"There … is another matter, Orilin. The Meldron sorceress, Umbra Lakar, is among the horde from the North. What higher power she serves is unknown."

"I've never heard of her before," said Orilin. "Except when we ran across her in the Dreath Wood."

"She is a new addition to the arsenal of Meldron sorcery, but a powerful one. Our scouts have been keeping track of the Meldron while you were away, seeing if they would re-emerge. Now that they have, especially a sorceress, we … have another request of you."

Orilin gazed at his friend.

"What is it, my liege?"

Lyrinias stared back at him with utmost seriousness.

"We want you to wield the Malanthar."

There was immediately some commotion in the throne room. The Malanthar was a sword which was forged in the Flame at Al-Nartha by Cyrus. It had been given to Alriad, king of Laerdiron to help fight off the Meldron during the first threat to the city. The Laerdiron Elves, armed with the weapon, had wrought a massive defeat upon the Meldron at the Battle of Rak-Mardan. The Meldron fled with terror back into the Mountains of Black and did not return for over a thousand years. Kal-Ardaan then gave the weapon to Talandrin, king of Caltirion to help fight off the Menetarrans at the Battle of Ithna. The Menetarrans were defeated, but Talandrin, in his greed, kept the weapon for himself. It was then that Laediron was overrun by the re-mustered Meldron. The exiled Elves never asked for the sword back. It had become a point of contention between Elvenkind and Caltirion. Talandrin, using it as his personal weapon, used it at the Battle of Targrin on the plains of Gallinthrar to try to capture the city-state. He was consumed by the Flame which came forth from the sword. From that day no king of Caltirion had dared to use it for any purpose but had kept it in a secret antechamber in the palace. It still kept the title of the "King's Sword" since only kings had used it.

"That weapon has not been used in over 300 years," said Orilin. "I dare not touch it."

"It can be wielded by those with noble purpose, Orilin," said Hhrin-Calin. "What is nobler than defending those you love?"

Larilyn came over to her husband.

"What is this 'Malanthar?'" she whispered.

"A terrible weapon," he said. "One that should not be used again."

The commotion in the crowd continued. Lyrinias held up his hands, and all went silent.

"Orilin, the Guard has come to me with the request that you indeed wield it. This host of enemies is possibly larger than Caltirion can handle. If Umbra Lakar and the Meldron join with these hosts from the south, we could be vastly outnumbered. It would spell doom for us."

Orilin reached for his wife's hand and squeezed it.

"I have no doubt of that, my liege," he said. "If you will, I would like to speak to my wife alone."

Lyrinias nodded.

"Of course."

Hhrin-Calin looked impatient. All eyes were watching the Elven couple as they left the throne room. Orilin led Larilyn into a small parlor outside the throne room.

"There is no avoiding it, love," he said.

Larilyn nodded.

"I know."

"You know I don't want a warrior's life anymore," he continued. "You know all I want to do is move back to that small cattle farm in Sargna with you. Live with you until we both Fade. But in order to have that dream I ..."

"You have to do this, Orilin," she said. "But neverthe-less, I go where you go. Remember that." He squeezed her hands.

"I know," he said. "Larilyn … People are going to die. I cannot stand back and just watch that happen. I cannot …"

"I know," she said. "Raltaron was right. You are an Elven warrior."

Orilin sighed.

"Not that I am so great," he said. "But … I cannot just … let this happen without ..."

"I know, love."

Orilin closed his eyes.

"Larilyn … I am re-enlisting in the Guard."

Larilyn nodded. Tears welled up in her eyes.

"Okay." she whispered.

Orilin stared deeply into her eyes.

"I love you, Larilyn. I do this for us, for the Kesstals, for … for Telbyrin."

They embraced.

Their embrace soon parted as Martralin entered and bid them come back into the throne room. They returned, where the whole court was waiting. Lyrinias walked forward.

"Well, brother. What say you?" Orilin looked to Lari-lyn and then to Lyrinias.

"I am re-enlisting in the Guard, my liege, if you will have me."

Commotion ran through the court again. Lyrinias raised his hands.

"You are most welcome, brother. Will you wield the King's Sword?"

There was silence through the whole room.

Orilin breathed deeply and looked back up at the king.

"I will." Lyrinias closed his eyes and smiled.

"So be it, Little Hawk. Welcome back to the Queen's Guard."

Chapter 12

THE NEXT MORNING ORILIN WAS LED BY KING Lyrinias, Hhrin-Calin, Martralin and Elrad down a flight of stone stairs behind the throne that led to an antechamber. It was a diamond-shaped room, dark blue in color and lit by four wall sconces. In the center of the room was a large golden eagle holding a dark blue sword in its talons. The sword itself had a pommel of golden eagle talons.

"I often come just to look at it," said Lyrinias. "I have never touched it in all my years." There was silence. The Malanthar gleamed in the torchlight.

"The King's Sword," said Orilin softly. Lyrinias smiled back at him.

"It is," he said. "Cyrus intended it to be such. To be shared by the kings of Telbyrin to defend good in the world." Orilin nodded. Shivers of fear ran through his blood.

"Only you have the right to touch it, Lyrinias."

The king looked to the sword and then to his friend.

"It is mine to give to whom I will," he said. "You, brother, are the King's champion now. I give it to you to wield for all of Telbyrin." Again there was silence.

"Are you afraid?" Lyrinias asked Orilin.

"Yes," he said.

Lyrinias smiled and put a hand on his friend's shoulder. Orilin looked to him and then to the sword. He slowly walked toward it, reached out his hand and stopped.

"The greedy cannot touch it!" breathed Orilin.

The other men looked to each other.

"Are you with greed, brother?" asked Lyrinias.

"Yes," sweated Orilin. "Such power. Such ..."

"Your heart is noble, Orilin," said Hhrin-Calin. "You do this for Telbyrin. You do not do this out of greed. Take it up."

Elrad walked over to Orilin whose hand was trembling.

"What do I do, father?" he asked. Elrad closed his eyes and put a hand on Orilin's shoulder.

"You do what you think is right, my son," he said. "If you take it, then do so. If not, then walk away."

Orilin started to sweat a little.

"I have to remember Talandrin's fate," he said.

Elrad turned him around.

"You are not Talandrin, my son," he said. "I know, if you choose to do so, that you take this weapon to defend those whom you love. Am I right?"

"Yes," said Orilin.

Elrad nodded.

"What is most dear to you, Orilin?"

He looked at him.

"Larilyn," he said. "My friends."

"You are already helping them by re-joining the Guard," Elrad said. "You hold these people with more value than your life. Why would you take up the sword then?"

Orilin looked back at the weapon.

"To strike fear into the heart of the Meldron and their sorcery."

Elrad's brow narrowed.

"A noble purpose, but not a good reason to take up the sword. What else?"

"Because the king wishes it," he continued.

"Obedience," said Elrad. "A greater purpose than the first. Now we are getting somewhere. What else?"

Orilin gasped.

"I don't know!"

"Yes you do," said Elrad.

Orilin breathed deeply.

"Because the people of Telbyrin need hope. The Flame is going out. People are panicking; living in fear. Families and lives are threatened now. They need hope!"

"Then take it up, son!" said Elrad strongly.

Orilin breathed rapidly.

"My Creator!" he shouted. He then laid his hand on the handle of the sword and freed it from the great eagle's talons. He held the weapon with both hands shaking and watched as an eerie blue flame enveloped the blade.

Orilin gasped. He held the sword, yet he was not consumed.

"The Flame healed you in Gallinthrar," said Elrad smiling. "I don't think it is going to consume you now."

Orilin looked at him. The blue flame soon went away and the blade gleamed in the torchlight. Lyrinias came up to his friend.

"Well done, brother!" he said embracing him from the side. Elrad stood in front of Orilin.

"Nothing will be able to break this weapon," he said. "Not even Meldron sorcery. The Flame will act in the blade as it wishes. Therefore always give it respect."

He went over to the other side of the antechamber and opened a safe. In it was a dark brown scabbard with a baldric.

"Keep it in this scabbard unless you have to use it," he continued. Orilin nodded. He was given the scabbard and he sheathed the weapon and slung it on his back.

"It has my utmost respect," said Orilin.

Elrad bowed and re-joined the king, Martralin and the Arch Vicar.

The four walked back up the stairs into the light again where Larilyn was waiting. Hhrin-Calin was clearly irritated with her, in his opinion, unwelcomed presence. She immediately saw Orilin with the sword.

"Orilin!" she said. "Is that it?"

He nodded.

"Yes, love. Everything is fine. Let's go for a walk shall we?"

Lyrinias came up to them.

"We do not have much time, brother," Lyrinias said. "Time is of the essence. I need you to report back in mid-afternoon."

Orilin bowed.

"Yes, my liege."

The king, Martralin and the Arch Vicar took their leave. Orilin looked over to Elrad.

"Will you walk with us, father?"

Elrad nodded. The three walked out in a little courtyard where a garden and fountain was. A statue of Queen Lorinthia was there. Also present was the old Elf Raltaron standing in the courtyard. Orilin and Larilyn were quite taken by surprise. Elrad looked to them.

"I better leave you alone with him," he said.

Orilin looked back as Elrad took his leave. Raltaron paced about.

"Queen Lorinthia!" he exclaimed. "Of whom the Guard was named after, as you know. Alrihon's beloved wife."

Orilin shook his head.

"We have much to discuss, Raltaron," he said.

The old Elf laughed.

"I imagine we do!"

"Why did you just leave us on the plains of Gallinthrar? We almost got killed back in Cedar Grove!"

"Well, that's an easy answer," he responded. "I could not just go through settlement after settlement carrying the Flame with me, could I? Not when the Vicar's are being hunted. The Meldron know about the Flame and their targets are the Vicars. If I just strode through town and said, 'Here I am!' wouldn't that have attracted attention? I've even heard that Menetarrans were in Cedar Grove. That wouldn't have been good would it?"

Orilin smirked.

"There is something you are not telling me."

Raltaron shrugged.

"Perhaps. But you need to know that I'm a special target of Umbra Lakar and her minions. I had to remain concealed."

"I would have protected you from that sorceress," said Orilin. "Besides, this Umbra Lakar had already ridden past the Wood when we met you. What you are telling me doesn't add up."

Raltaron smirked and cleared his throat.

"I could not have gone through Cedar Grove with the Flame, son! I could not have the Menetarrans report to Umbra of my whereabouts. Now … are you satisfied?"

Orilin glared at him and then rolled his eyes.

"Whatever."

"Come walk with me," said Raltaron.

Orilin and Larilyn followed him up a long flight of stairs to a tower atop the palace.

"The whole world seems to be before us," said Larilyn.

Raltaron looked to her and smiled.

"How right you are my little girl on the ranch!"

Larilyn leered at him.

"At least it's an honest job. More honest than subterfuge and hiding secrets."

Raltaron laughed.

"I like you my little seasonal harvester. It's good that you have your Elven jocularity back."

Orilin sneered at him.

"Really," continued Raltaron. "There are more things in this world that you two farmstead punches know -- at least … as of yet."

"Enlighten us, crotchety cleric," said Orilin.

Raltaron looked over to him.

"Whoa! That was a good one! I kind of like this charming little game of name-calling. But as much as I wish to carry on, I must alas motion to adjourn. Aghmm. Where was I? Oh, yes. There are things in this world that are unknown to you that will be shown to you."

"Why not now?" asked Orilin flatly.

"Because frankly, Orilin, now is not the time. Seriously, if Elves can recover to seriousness properly, which I believe that they can, you can believe me when I say that these matters will be shown to you when and where they will be shown to you. But I can promise that they will be shown to you … when they will be shown to you."

Orilin and Larilyn just looked at each other.

"Whatever, Raltaron," said Orilin. "I've frankly seen enough for today."

Raltaron looked at him grimly.

"Today is far from over, Orilin. But I'd say we are done here for now, don't you?"

Orilin nodded.

"At least we have clarified why you just left us after the Dreath Wood."

Raltaron laughed and started to walk back down the stairs.

"I will be here, Master Orilin," he said. "We will speak again soon." With that he walked down the stairs and left them atop the tower. Orilin looked to his wife and then forward into the distance; his bluish-black hair blowing in the wind.

"They get closer," he said.

Larilyn looked out as well.

"I know. How can they be stopped?"

Orilin sighed.

"I don't know. I feel like we are stuck here. I guess we are."

"What do you mean?" asked Larilyn.

"Well," he continued, "I want to help, and I want to help now. But there are strategies and maneuvers that must be planned in war. I leave that to the king and the commander of the Caltirion army. I am here to serve. But I wish we could get on with it."

Larilyn squeezed his hand tight.

"You will, love. But don't leave me for war too fast."

Orilin looked at her and smiled.

"So what do you want to do until mid-afternoon?"

She smiled.

"Play for me."

ᛉ ᛉ ᛉ ᛉ ᛉ ᛉ

Orilin was given a new harp, and he played for his wife. The music made him feel good as well; much more so than the feasting and court. It was not so long that there was a sharp knock at their door.

"Orilin," said a voice.

His fingers stopped in mid-song.

"Yes?"

"King Lyrinias requests your presence outside imme-diately."

Orilin got up from his seat, put the harp down, kissed Larilyn, and went to the door.

"How may I be of service to his Majesty?" he asked Captain Aldanar, who was standing at the door.

"Come with me."

Orilin followed him into a room where Lyrinias, Hhrin-Calin, Elrad and Martralin were.

"Thank you, Master Orilin, for coming with haste," said Hhrin-Calin.

Orilin nodded.

"What can I do, your Reverence?"

Hhrin-Calin pointed to a map of the North on a table.

"We are planning our first strike against the Mene-tarrans. We have sent scouts of the Guard traveling south toward Sargna in order to report back to us what is going on there."

"We need you to help lead the first strike at Gallinthrar," said Lyrinias. "We promised Captain Hadar aid."

Orilin nodded.

"I know. I am glad to do it. Will Captain Aldanar help lead the strike as well?"

Lyrinias shook his head.

"Aldanar is needed elsewhere."

"My liege, may I ask why?" asked Orilin. "The full brunt of the attack is happening in Gallinthrar right now. The Guard will need their Captain."

Lyrinias nodded.

"We will discuss this in court, which will be held soon."

About an hour later Orilin and Larilyn were led into the throne room were the Queen and dignitaries were present. The whole unit of the Guard that stationed the palace was present there. The room was filled with people almost to the point of being uncomfortable, but the crowd made room for the two Elves. Captain Aldanar stood by the King and Queen.

"Welcome, Orilin. Lady Larilyn," said Lyrinias.

The two bowed to the king.

"My liege," said Orilin. "When will we get underway?"

Lyrinias and Aldanar came down from the throne to meet him.

"Very soon, my friend," said the king. "In fact, almost immediately. We have one more item to address here. The army of Caltirion awaits outside. The whole Guard awaits. Captain Aldanar."

The Captain came forward.

"My lord," he said to Orilin. "My men respect you. Master Martralin was your teacher and Elrad your father. You served in her Majesty's Guard for almost 100 years; far more than any life of a Human Captain. In it your loyalty was without question and your valor exceptional. Now you wield the greatest weapon in Telbyrin: the Malanthar. And you wield it to defend others without greed or reason for personal gain. Again, you come to us with exceptional valor. My lord Orilin, I release my position to you as Captain of the Guard."

Many people stirred at this, but were quickly silent. Orilin was stunned.

"My lord Aldanar," he said. "I have rejoined the Guard but certainly do not request this honor."

Lyrinias stepped forward.

"It is my wish as well, Lord Orilin," he said. "I have spoken at length to Captain Aldanar about this. It is my wish that you take command of the Lorinthian Guard."

Orilin knew now that he could not get out of this.

"I do not wish this honor," said Orilin. "But if this is his Majesty's wish, then I will obey."

Aldanar stepped forward extending his arm. Orilin clasped it and bowed his head. Aldanar then took a knee.

"I pledge undying obedience to you, my Captain," he said. "Only his and her Majesty do I hold higher than you."

Orilin lifted him up and put a hand on his shoulder.

"To the death for her Majesty," said Orilin in the ancient pledge of fealty of the Lorinthian Guard.

"To the death for her Majesty," said Aldanar.

The rest of the Guard came forward and pledged fealty to Orilin who one by one was embraced by him. Lyrinias and Queen Lirana smiled at each other, watching the ceremony. After its completion, Lyrinias stepped forward.

"Well done, Captain Orilin," he said. "Now let me give you my blessing. Kneel."

Orilin did so.

"In the name of Alrihon the Great and Queen Lorinthia and in my own name, you Orilin Alandiron are hereby Captain of her Majesty's Guard, Caltirion's most prized fighting force. And I grant you all the rights and privileges of such. I hereby proclaim that in Caltirion's fighting forces, there is no other higher than yourself. Besides myself and her Majesty, none of the Guard will hold any higher than you. To the death for her Majesty!"

Orilin closed his eyes.

"To the death for her Majesty!" yelled all the Guard.

Lyrinias took Orilin by the forearm.

"Arise, Captain Orilin Alandiron."

The crowd erupted in applause, which continued for some time. He rejoined Larilyn at her side. She took his hand and squeezed it.

"That sounded official," she said low to him.

Orilin smiled.

"It was very official."

Queen Lirana came up to Larilyn.

"Lady Larilyn, I wish to give you my blessing. Kneel."
Larilyn, a little confused, did so.

"Larilyn Alandiron, wife of the Captain of the Queen's Guard, Orilin Alandiron, I give you all the rights, titles and privileges of a lady of the realm of Hallintor. Henceforth you shall no longer be known as Larilyn but Dame Larilyn. Arise."

Larilyn arose and bowed to the queen.

"I am grateful to her Majesty," she replied, not knowing what else to say. The queen bowed back and rejoined her husband. She made a motion with her hand and Iomil came forward.

"Iomil,' said the queen. "I honorably appoint you as Dame Larilyn's maidservant. Do you accept?"

"I most graciously accept, your Majesty," she replied. The queen nodded and Iomil bowed and joined Larilyn at her side.

"Dame Larilyn," she said. "I am henceforth your most humble servant."

Larilyn smiled.

"I wanted no other."

The two Elf women embraced.

"You will have to help me get use to this," said Larilyn. "Being a lady and all."

They both smiled. The crowd went into applause again. Orilin went up to his wife and bowed to her and kissed her hand. She blushed.

"My darling wife," he said. She embraced him. Lyrinias smiled.

"We are adjourned," he said to the court. "Captain Orilin has a long evening and night ahead of him." Everyone bowed to him as they went out. Lyrinias came up to Orilin.

"Come with me, Captain," he said. Martralin and Elrad followed. Orilin quickly turned to his wife.

"Wait for me in our chambers, my lady," he said.

Larilyn smirked. All of a sudden things were not normal anymore. No longer were they the farm couple in Sargna. They were a lord and lady. Deep down, she wanted the normal back.

"Okay," she said.

"Yes, my lord," Iomil whispered in her ear. Larilyn looked at him.

"Ah … yes, my lord."

Orilin smiled and her and winked. Her nervousness ebbed away.

Chapter 13

THE KING AND HIS DIGNITARIES LED ORILIN INTO a small armory. In it were weapons, shields and armor of all shapes and sizes. Elrad had for Orilin a short shirt and shorts. At Elrad's bidding, Orilin removed his robe and put them on privately. He knew what was about to happen. He held out his arms and spread his legs apart a little.

Elrad and Martralin put armor on him. Silver bracers were placed on his arms and silver greaves on his legs. Lastly, a silver breastplate with a hawk's head on the front was placed on him. Orilin looked down and smiled.

"It was made for you," said Elrad. Then a silver-plumed helmet was fitted on him.

"You may choose a spear and shield, Captain," said Lyrinias. Orilin went over to the shields and chose a customary circular one. It was light, but very strong. He then went over to the spears and chose the heaviest one for his weight. He hefted it a bit and then put it down.

"These will do fine, my liege," he said.

Elrad came forward.

"You look grand, my son," he said. "Allow me to carry your helmet for you." Orilin did so and they left the armory.

When they came out, Aldanar met them.

"My liege," he said. "The Menetarrans have launched full assault on Gallinthrar."

The king nodded.

"As I have expected. Have the men assemble at the south gate for deployment. On Captain Orilin's command, we march. Aldanar saluted and rushed off to complete the command. Lyrinias turned to the Captain.

"Captain," he said. "Assemble the Guard. I only want one unit to protect the palace. Understood?"

"Yes, my liege," said Orilin.

"You may bid your wife goodbye," said the king. "Tonight, we ride for war." Orilin saluted and went to his chambers.

He entered fully armored. Larilyn was sitting in her recliner looking out to the south. Iomil was tending to her hair. When Iomil saw Orilin, she bowed and left the room. Larilyn ran to her husband and the two embraced. She looked down at his armor.

"You look handsome," she said softly.

He smiled.

"Hopefully I will have to wear it rarely. Larilyn, listen to me!"

She looked at him.

"I want you to know that we are still Orilin and Larilyn Alandiron, farmers of Sargna on the Kesstal ranch." Tears started to well up in her eyes.

"I'm afraid, love," she said.

"I know," he replied. "Don't be. Listen. I ride to war right now. Pray for me, for us and for the Kesstals. Whatever happens, stay close to Iomil. If the Menetarrans breach Gallinthrar, they will head for Caltirion. They shouldn't though. Creator willing, we will crush them where they stand."

Larilyn held his hands tightly.

"I don't want you to ride to war, love," she whispered. Orilin nodded.

"I know. I don't either. But you still trust me, don't you?"

Larilyn nodded and touched one of his ears. Orilin smiled.

"Things will be well again, love," he said. The two met in a kiss and then he turned to leave.

"Orilin!" she cried.

"Yes, love."

"I love you."

He smiled.

"I love you too."

$$\gamma\gamma\gamma\gamma\gamma\gamma$$

It was late afternoon when they rode out. Orilin rode on one of the chariots that belonged to the commander of the army.

"There will be many, Captain," the commander said to Orilin. "And they will be strong."

Orilin nodded.

"Let us stick to our original plan," said Orilin. "The Guard and the infantry will draw the brunt of the attack. Send the cavalry to flank them. Gallinthrar's forces will aid the Guard."

The commander nodded.

They reached Gallinthrar that night. The cavalry had long since tailed off from the shock troops and the Guard from Caltirion. As the infantry and the Guard reached the top of the hill they saw it; the horde of the Menetarrans. They were laying siege to the city proper and fire could be seen in the distance. Torla and some other cavalry from Gallinthrar met the Guard and the Caltirion infantry.

"Lord Orilin!" said Torla. "Thank the Creator you are here! We are holding them back, but we can't hold on for much longer. There are too many of them."

Orilin stepped forward and unsheathed the Malanthar. It gleamed with the Flame. Torla and his men stepped back and gasped.

"We are here to answer them, Lord Torla!" said Orilin.

"With Caltirion's finest and the King's Sword!" All the men cheered and banged their shields with their spears.

Orilin raised the Malanthar high.

"Let them hear you, men!" yelled Orilin. The shouts grew louder and Torla looked on in amazement. He lighted from his horse and walked up to Orilin.

"The King's Sword has not been used in over 300 years," he said. "And now you wield it! We honor your presence among us."

Orilin smiled and put a hand on Torla's shoulder.

"It is an honor for us to be here," he said. He then turned to his men.

"This night is not just about one Elven warrior!" he shouted. "This night is about all of us and all of Telbyrin. These brutes think that the Flame has been snuffed out among us. These brutes think that they can have whatever they want: our land, our wives, our children. Now, let us take terror to them!"

He paced down the flanks.

"Men! I do not see men with undivided hearts. I see men who hold creed, country and loved ones higher than life itself. We do not fight for gold or land or anything tonight that fades away. We fight for what lasts. The Flame is not just an outward symbol. The Flame is in our hearts! So go show it to them!"

The men roared and banged shields again.

"Men of Caltirion! Form ranks!"

The men shouted and formed their ranks.

"Guard! Form ranks!" continued Orilin. "To the death for her Majesty!"

"To the death for her Majesty!" the Guard shouted.

Orilin held the Malanthar high.

"For Hallintor! And for Telbyrin!" Then there was a deafening roar of the men. Orilin commanded the charge. The men charged the field toward the Menetarran horde. The plan was working so far. Part of the horde took its concentration off Gallinthrar and concentrated on the advancing Caltirion ranks.

They kept running until Orilin saw Menetarran archers in the distance.

"Shields up!" commanded Orilin.

The entire ranks were covered with the iron circular shields, and the men advanced slowly. The Menetarran archers began to fire. Arrows shattered against the shields and a few men were hit in the legs and feet.

"Forward!" yelled Orilin. More arrows rained down upon the shields. Orilin looked between the shields for a chance to strike but the archers were too far away still.

"Guard!" he shouted. "Break from infantry!" The Guard did so to take the archers' concentration off the whole mass. More arrows. A few of the Guard went down.

"Forward!" yelled Orilin. "Fast!" The Guard hopped to a chant of yells faster toward the Menetarran ranks. Orilin now saw their chance.

"Break ranks and strike!" The Guard broke ranks and struck into the heart of the Menetarran ranks. The commander of the infantry ordered them to follow up and reinforce the Guard.

Orilin dove right into them. The Malanthar was still gleaming. He bashed his shield into one foe and tore through the throat of another. One by one he mowed them down with the King's Sword. The foes around him ran when they saw the Flame but the Guard did not let them escape. Several Menetarrans were nailed to the ground by spears from the hands of the Guard.

Orilin went into a horrific deathly dance. He carved through one Menetarran after another. Several of them ran up to him and tried to attack but he fended them off. Each one of them was killed in return. One threw his spear at him. Orilin dodged, struck and sliced through the throat. One attacked him with a hammer. Orilin blocked it with his shield and impaled the man. He wrenched his sword out and sliced through the kneecap of another. He then mowed two more down, came over to the man with the maimed knee and impaled him. One large Menetarran ran toward him.

"Spear!" shouted Orilin. An Elven Guard tossed him

a spear and Orilin slung it toward his attacker and nailed him to the ground. He wrenched the Malanthar from his impaled foe.

The Caltirion infantry were next to strike. They struck the Menetarrans from the south. The Menetarrans briefly took their concentration off the Guard and attacked the on-coming Caltirion army. Orilin saw his chance.

"Guard!" he shouted. "Form ranks!" They did so and raised their shields.

"Attack from behind!" The Guard struck from behind and crushed the rear of the Menetarran horde. The horde was sandwiched in-between them and the Caltirion infantry.

"Crush them!" yelled Orilin. The Menetarrans were helpless. It was then an all-out slaughter. The Guard im-paled them with their spears and the Malanthar was drenched in blood. The barbarians began to flee for their lives while still being mowed down. Then Caltirion's cavalry struck from the hill raining arrows down upon the fleeing Menetarrans. More barbarians fell and the cavalry pursued them to the last man.

"Guard!" yelled Orilin. "Form ranks!" The men did so. Torla and his men had broken from the fighting and rendez-voused with them.

"I will lead you to the gates!" said Torla. "There are more on the way!"

The Guard and the infantry were led into the gates of Gallinthrar while the cavalry took up position on a distant hill. When they were in, Captain Hadar came to meet them.

"Lord Orilin!" he yelled. Orilin took off his helmet and saluted Hadar.

"Captain Hadar," he said. "We have broken their ranks."

Hadar nodded.

"I knew you would recover from that wound!" he said embracing Orilin. "Come. We will treat your wounded."

The men went to wash up, drink or have their wounds treated. Orilin walked with Captain Hadar.

"Torla tells me there are more on the way," he said.
Hadar nodded.

"Yes. I am glad his Majesty has kept his word. They will be badly shaken now, but they will return."

"Then the wall must hold," said Orilin.

Hadar nodded.

"Come with me."

Captain Hadar led Orilin into a room atop one of the towers on the battlements. In it were the military commanders of Gallinthrar. When they saw Orilin they stopped what they were doing and saluted. Orilin returned the salute.

"Orilin Alandiron?" one asked.

The Elf nodded.

"You have come just in time," another said.

Orilin joined them at the table.

"We have," he said. "And the Guard is still in good spirit."

One man came forward clad in bronze armor and a red cloak.

"I am Commander Hadix," he said. "Commander of Gallinthrar's forces."

Orilin bowed.

"Orilin Alandiron. Captain of Her Majesty's Guard." Some of the men looked at each other.

"No offense, Captain," said Commander Hadix. "But I thought Captain Aldanar was still in command."

Orilin nodded.

"He was. But at his bidding and his Majesty's bidding they have given the command over to me. Believe me I did not want this honor. It was enough for me to rejoin the Guard. But apparently not enough for his Majesty."

"Apparently," said Hadix. "Congratulations, Captain Orilin."

Orilin raised his head.

"Thank you, Commander. How may we be of further service to Gallinthrar?"

Hadix looked to his men and then back to Orilin.

"We would request his Majesty to allow the Caltirion infantry and the Guard to help protect these battlements from the rest of the Menetarran horde."

"I cannot speak for the Commander of the infantry, but the Guard will stay and fight," said Orilin.

Hadix nodded.

"We are trying to devise why they are attacking in the first place, Captain Orilin."

Orilin looked to the Commander.

"When my wife and I were traveling to Caltirion, we crossed paths with Barras Drin and a Meldron sorceress named Umbra Lakar. We remained unseen but overheard some of their plans. They mentioned they were riding south and that the Menetarrans were riding north towards Gallinthrar. It's a distraction likely."

"A distraction from what?"

"From where the sorceress and Barras Drin will likely be striking. Commander Hadix, I believe the real battle does not concern Gallinthrar and Caltirion, but Al-Nartha."

"They wouldn't dare," said Hadix. "The Meldron especially wouldn't strike the Temple of the Flame!"

"The Flame is going out, Commander," said Orilin. "And we still don't know why." There was a silence.

"Why else would they be riding south?" asked Orilin. "Commander, both cities have to find some way to help defend Al-Nartha when this affair with your city and Caltirion is all over. The more I have thought about this the more it makes sense. Vicar Raltaron told me that more would be revealed to me in time. The Menetarrans don't care about religious matters in this case. They care about reaping the riches of Gallinthrar and Hallintor. They are a distraction, most likely. The lords of the Meldron want to route the Vicars and snuff out the Flame. I've read the ancient scrolls when I was a boy under Elrad. King Ralharin battled Cyrus. Cyrus defeated him. Then the Meldron awoke from time to time after that, and every time the Elves routed them. Then there was the fall of Laerdiron; something the world believed it would never see. Now 300 years later, we have this. If my guess is true, this will be larger than the fall of Laerdiron. This is an attack on all of Telbyrin."

Again there was a silence.

"What is the Meldron's purpose in doing all this?" asked Hadix.

At that instant walked in the Vicar Lau.

"To envelope the world in their doctrine of Darkness," he said. "To reveal to the world their doctrine of the Eternal Secret and to fulfill the ancient wishes of King Ralharin."

All eyes were on the Vicar. Orilin then looked to the Commander.

"The Vicar seems to agree with me, Commander."

"Yes," said Lau. "Captain Orilin is wise in this respect. Commander, our scouts from the east have reported Meldron troops marching from the Mountains of Black."

"Towards where?" asked Hadix.

"Towards Caltirion," said Lau.

Orilin looked down. There was a long silence.

"This was well planned by them for some time," said Hadix. "The world was unfortunately complacent."

"Yes," said Orilin. "As I have said, they are distracting us."

Hadix nodded.

"Captain Orilin, I take you at your word. What is your wish?"

In walked Commander Lardin, commander of Caltirion's infantry.

"Captain Orilin," he said. "My men are in high spirits but are still being tended to. Is there any report of a possible future attack?"

Orilin looked to him.

"Commander, we have another problem in Caltirion."

"What is it, my lord?" he asked.

"Vicar Lau says that there are enemy troops from the Mountains of Black coming towards the city."

Commander Lardin's brow narrowed.

"Can the defenses of Gallinthrar hold?"

"They will hold," said Commander Hadix. "Go and defend Caltirion."

"Commander," Lardin began, "I don't mean to question your judgment, but what if an even larger force approaches your city?"

"Our defenses will hold, Commander," said Hadix. "Go and defend your king."

Orilin looked to Hadix.

"I and the remaining Guard here will help hold Gallinthrar; if that is acceptable to you, Commander."

"It is acceptable," he replied. "Are the king's defenses suitable?"

"I believe they are," said Orilin. "But I must return to Caltirion when we are done here. I must see to my wife."

"Understood," said Hadix. "I will see ready the siege engines for another strike. Commander Lardin, go and dismiss your infantry."

"Yes, my lord," he replied. He went over to Orilin.

"Will you come with me, Captain, and help me gather up my men?"

"Yes," said Orilin. He then grabbed Lardin by his forearm.

"When you reach Caltirion you must tell my wife that I have not forgotten about her! Tell her that I come straight there after this is all over!"

"I swear it!" replied Lardin.

Orilin went among the many troops of Caltirion and Gallinthrar. Already they were preparing for the next attack. Commander Hadix was already letting his men know what was taking place.

"Infantry!' yelled Commander Lardin. "Form ranks!" Some of the men looked questionably at each other but obeyed. Orilin went among some of the wounded infantry telling them that they were going home. One young Elf lay on his side. He was recovering from an arrow wound to the thigh. He looked up at Orilin.

"Are we going home, Captain Orilin?"

Orilin knelt down beside him.

"You are," he said. "But the Guard stays."

The Elf looked confused.

"Why does the infantry leave in the midst of battle, my lord?"

Orilin sighed.

"Because Caltirion will be under attack soon."

The Elf leaned up.

"Under attack? From who?"

Orilin bid him lay back down.

"Relax," he said. "What is your name?"

"Oandor, my lord," he said.

"You will go to the physicians, Oandor," said Orilin.

The Elf lay back down and chuckled a bit.

"What is it?" asked Orilin.

Oandor looked back at him.

"It's just that, my lord, my beloved is a physician. I am going to ask her hand in marriage soon. I believe she is my soulmate. I only hope to live to experience my life with her."

Orilin smiled.

"What is her name? Your beloved?"

"Iomil, my lord." Orilin's eyes widened.

"Iomil is my wife's maidservant. When you return, tell your beloved to tell my wife that I am well. Can you do that for me?" Oandor nodded.

"I swear it, my lord." Orilin put a hand on his shoulder.

"May the Creator bless you and Iomil, Oandor."

"Thank you, my lord Orilin." He was then carried away on a stretcher.

Chapter 14

ELIMED LED THEM THROUGH MORE THICKETS AND PAST streams not believing what he saw. Acaida was overrun and people had fled. The last thing he wanted was the Kesstals to be part of it. Many of the citizens of Acaida were doing exactly what Elimed was doing. Going into the Niodath Forests, where the Wood Fays dwelt. Indeed, most of them had no other alternative. Zitha and Alanna followed closely behind the Vicar.

"I want Larilyn!" said Alanna. "I hope she is okay."

Zitha looked back at her.

"If I know anything about Orilin and Larilyn, dear, they are just fine. Now let's keep going. We will be safe in these forests."

Zitha never thought she would live to say those words. Drelas held his father's hand.

"I'm scared, father," he said.

"Of what?" replied Alander.

"Of the Wood Fays. What if they eat children and don't love them?"

Alander picked up his pace.

"You're picking up on too much of that Elven humor from friends," he said. "Courage."

Drelas squeezed his hand.

Elimed and the Kesstals had more Acaidans following them. There were about 24 total and who knew how many more in the forest? They crossed another stream. In it was crystal clear water and had black and grey fish swimming in it. Elimed led them across stepping stones.

"Come now," he said. "We will need to settle before nightfall." They crossed the stream and came up into very thick, tall trees with moss and tendrils all over them.

"Now, we will start to get deep," said Elimed. "Keep your eyes fixed on me and the path I lead you down. Don't venture off."

Elimed led them between the trees and deeper into the forests. Nothing now could be heard except the crickets and some owls way off in the distance. Elimed led them for about a half hour more then stopped in front of three massive trees.

"Come out, you sprites!" he yelled. "The Flame is in danger. We need your Vicar and your Queen!"

There was a long awkward silence. Again Elimed yelled.

"Zarkaia! We are sorry to disturb you and your little …"

Arrows were then pointed at them from all directions. A large mossy net was thrown over Elimed and the Kesstals. They were pulled up a bit and Alanna screamed.

"Great, Elimed!" said Alander. "Now you're probably going to get us killed."

Elimed struggled a bit.

"Let us down. I am a Vicar of the Flame!"

Two figures strode before them. They were clad in mossy garments and their skin was green. They were the height of large children and their eyes were bright yellow. They had tawny hair. One was male and the other was female. The female wore long hair with leaves in it.

"We have seen the forests flooded with Humans and Elves," said the male. "Who are you?"

"I am Elimed of Acaida, you dirty little sprite," he said. "Now let us down and lead us to Zarkaia."

"Don't make demands of them, Elimed," said Alander.
The female strode forward.

"I am Kala and this is Gert," she said. "We are the protectors of this part of the forest. We will lead you to our queen, but you are all our prisoners now."

Elimed scoffed.

"Let me see Nalin, your Vicar," he said. "We know of him, though I have never met him."

"No more demands," said Kala. "Gert, cut them loose."

The Fay obeyed and cut the top of the net. The prisoners all spilled out. Alanna and Drelas brushed the leaves out of their hair. The Fays backed up.

"More children!" gasped Gert. "So many of them now!"

Alander spoke up.

"Please, they are mine," he said. "The Vicar is right. Sargna has been overrun by barbarians and your forests were the only place we could retreat to. We are friends of Orilin Alandiron."

Gert's eyes widened, then he slowly smiled.

"Ha, ha, ha!" he laughed.

"What?" yelled Alander. "He is our friend."

"He is," said Alanna. "Please, Mister Gert. Please. I promise I know Orilin. I promise."

Gert slowly bent down to her and smiled.

"Have you ever met the Fay Queen, little one?"

Alanna looked up into his bright yellow eyes.

"No, sir," she said.

"Your friend the Little Hawk has. Come, you will meet her."

The Wood Fays bound their prisoners with mossy tendrils except for the children. Gert and Kala took the lead. They had taken all the people from Acaida prisoner and led them deeper through the dark forests. Alanna could see more yellowy eyes peering at them from the large trees. The owls kept hooting in the distance and the crickets still sang. It was getting dark. Alander came up to Elimed.

"What's your grand plan now?"

The Vicar snickered.

"We're their prisoners now. Not much I can do except do what they say. Zarkaia should help sort out things. So there is not much planned on this end."

Just then there was an almost obnoxious but funny song coming from trees. The voices sounded almost like children's. Alanna and Drelas saw more yellow eyes.

Wood Fays by the dozen started merrily jumping out of the trees. They ran up playfully to the prisoners.

"Ah, prisoners!" they shouted. "All shapes and sizes. Children too!"

Zitha was getting more nervous by the second. The silly song began to increase in volume and intensity. Elimed was embarrassed that they would dare to take a Vicar prisoner. He went up to Gert.

"Mister Gert, when and if we meet Nalin, I will have words with him."

"Ha, ha ha!" laughed Gert. "Just you wait."

"What are they singing about, Elimed?" asked Alanna.

"They are obviously getting excited about something," said Elimed. "I wager that …"

Just then there was laughing all around, and two figures jumped out of the trees. One was a female Fay who was a little taller than the rest. She, like the others, had green skin, yellow eyes and tawny hair. Next to her was a short male Fay. He was somewhat skinny and had a funny pointed nose. He was clad in a leaf tunic and breechcloth. In his hands he held a piece of the Flame.

"Ah, Vicar Nalin!" said Elimed. "It must be you!" The Fay smiled.

"I am Nalin indeed!" he said bombastically. "I heard mention of a Vicar being captured and I brought the Flame for you to touch … to test if you are really a Vicar. Good luck!"

The Wood Fays laughed. Elimed could not believe what he was hearing.

"Why … allow me to see the Flame!" he said. "I have proof of my ordination."

"How did they find out so fast about you, Elimed?" asked Alander.

"Word travels fast among the Fay," answered the female. "Allow me to introduce myself to you. I am Zarkaia; Queen of the Forests."

All the Fay bowed a little. There was a silence.

"Touch the Flame, Elimed," said Zarkaia.

Elimed was in a way scandalized.

"I will. But it is cruel to just ask someone to go up and touch the Flame. It can both heal and destroy."

"Isn't your heart pure, Master Elimed?" asked Zarkaia. "Go ahead."

Elimed scoffed, and Gert untied his bonds. Elimed strode over to Vicar Nalin and picked up the Flame. He reverently held it aloft his head for all the Fay to see. They all cheered. He handed it back to Nalin.

"I thought as much," commented Nalin. "Well done."

Zarkaia went up to Elimed and the Kesstals.

"Like I said, word travels fast among the Fay. When Gert and Kala found you, word flew through the forest. The name Orilin Alandiron was mentioned." She looked at Alanna.

"You said you know him, young one?"

Alanna nodded.

"Yes … my Lady. He and his wife, Larilyn, live on our farm."

Zarkaia laughed.

"So he did marry! I thought that would never happen."

"Why?" asked Alanna.

Zarkaia laughed again.

"When he was around 150 years old he was a notorious adventurer. Oh, I remember him when he came to the forest. We imprisoned him, but he escaped.

"He showed so much talent for a young Elf, and he was already a master swordsman before he joined this Guard people speak of in the Outer Lands. I tried to keep him in the forests and make him my husband, but he refused. He said he had not found his soulmate. Some Elven concept. I tried to force him but he escaped me. Ha, ha! I take it this Larilyn is his soulmate?"

Alanna smiled.

"Oh, she is. She is a really beautiful Elf and knows how to work the farm well."

Zarkaia laughed again.

"He married a farm girl?! I always thought he would win the hand of some noblewoman in far-off lands. Is he okay?"

"Yes," said Alanna. "When he returns, I'm going to learn the pipes from him. Larilyn is going to make me an Elf too – put Elven yarn in my hair and all. Would you like to hear me play?"

Zarkaia chuckled.

"Why yes, Alanna," she said. "That would be quite nice."

Alanna took off her pipes from around her neck. She started to play. It wasn't a grand melody by any means but the Fay were enjoying it nonetheless. When she finished, she looked up at Zarkaia.

"How did I do, my Lady?" she asked. Zarkaia smiled.

"You did grand, my darling. Come, all of you can stay in the trees with us tonight. You will be safe in the forests."

Zitha and Alander's bonds were untied and they rushed over to their children.

"I enjoyed your daughter's tune," said Zarkaia to Zitha. "You will now be received as our guests."

Zitha nervously nodded.

The Fays jumped back up in the trees. Gert and Kala tied mossy ropes to the Acaidans' waists.

"You may want to become an Elf," said Zarkaia to Alanna, "But you cannot climb like a Fay. Hold on!" Alanna did so. They were all pulled up into the trees with incredible speed. Alanna screamed, then suddenly realized that she was in a tree-house with the Fay Queen.

"That was incredible!" she said to Zarkaia.

The Fay Queen chuckled.

"You need to rest," she said.

Alanna nodded.

"Do you believe me about Orilin, my Lady?"

Zarkaia eyed her.

"Yes, darling," she said. "Now go rest."

Alanna and her family tried to rest in the Fay tree houses, which were almost part of the trees. Alander and Zitha had an especially difficult time trying to sleep. Elimed, however, was not allowed to sleep. He was summoned by Nalin and Queen Zarkaia.

They went out on one of the tallest trees in the grove. It overlooked the vast forest. The moon and the stars shone brightly.

"What is this about the Flame?" asked Nalin. "The rest of the Fays said you said it was in danger."

Elimed nodded.

"Where did you put the piece of the Flame, Nalin?"

Nalin looked up at him.

"I put it in one of our Sanctuaries. It's not 'out' as you say. How could it go out?"

"I don't know," said Elimed. Orilin, Larilyn and the Kesstal family stopped in Acaida in Sargna on their way to Al-Nartha."

The Fays looked at each other. They knew nothing about Sargna or Acaida, but they did know about Al-Nartha. All they really knew were their forests.

"Anyway," continued Elimed. "The piece of the Flame that was housed in the Acaida Sanctuary went out. I sent Orilin and Larilyn to a great king in the Outer Lands named Lyrinias. The Arch-Vicar was going to be there too. They were to seek answers from them. I myself wanted to go, but they convinced me not to. They said I needed to stay here for the people of Acaida, so I stayed. I don't know what is going on in the world, but it must be bad. What am I saying?! It is bad! That's why we came into the Great Forests. Acaida was overrun by barbarians from Menetarra. They plundered the city. Those who survived made their way into this forest."

Zarkaia stared at him.

"Some of us took escaping soldiers prisoner," she said.

"Did you take everyone prisoner?!" asked Elimed.

"Yes," said Zarkaia. "You trespassed into our forests."

"Don't you believe my story?!" he replied. "The Flame is going out, and we were overrun! We had to seek refuge in the forests!"

Zarkaia nodded. Nalin walked up.

"The Flame has certainly not gone out here," he said. "Why should we believe you? Some of us, the Queen among us, were going to Al-Nartha ourselves for pilgrimage."

"I wouldn't do that," said Elimed. "Al-Nartha and the Vicars could be a target."

"Why would you say that?" asked Nalin.

"I swear upon my ordination that the Flame went out, Nalin!"

There was a silence. Zarkaia looked up.

"If what you say is really true, Elimed, you need to remain in the forests. I will go to Al-Nartha to see for myself what is going on."

"Why?" huffed Elimed. "You too could be a target?!"

"By whom?" asked the Fay Queen.

"By Meldron!" The two Fays looked at each other and back to Elimed.

"How do you know they are involved?"

"It's only a guess on my part," said Elimed. "But if something wrong is going on with the Flame, then they should be involved."

"You just say that because they are your arch-enemy." Elimed shook his head.

"I say that because the history tells of the Meldron wanting to do such a thing. In the Chronicles of Laerdiron it tells of their king Ralharin wanting to snuff the Flame out."

The Fay Queen looked at him curiously.

"You have my leave to take refuge in the forests," she said. "Get some rest."

Zarkaia and Nalin then left Elimed and went off to talk by themselves.

"Come with me to Al-Nartha," said Zarkaia.

"Yes, my Queen," said Nalin. "I am most curious about what is taking place."

"We need to be ready for anything," said the queen. "I do not believe Elimed is a liar."

"Nor do I," said Nalin, "Although I was skeptical at first. But when a Vicar swears upon his ordination, that is most serious."

"Yes," said Zarkaia. "Do not talk about this much. We need to leave as soon as we can."

Chapter 15

LARILYN STOOD ON HER BALCONY FROM HER CHAMBERS looking towards Gallinthrar. She saw the smoke rising from the valley
and worried much if her beloved was still alive. Iomil walked
in.

"My lady looks very stressed," she said. Larilyn
looked back to her.

"To say the least," she said in reply. Iomil came over
to her and stood by her.

"If I know anything about your husband, if all I heard
of him is correct, he will come back to you."

Larilyn nodded.

"I guess I need some rest," she said. "I've been
standing here for hours. There is nothing to do either but
walk around these parts of the palace."

"It is safe for you, my lady," she replied.

Larilyn nodded again.

"I suppose you are right. I just wish I could do something. Something to help."

Iomil smiled slightly.

"You need your rest, my lady. I will be here if you
need me."

"Thank you, Iomil," said Larilyn.

Larilyn went up to her chambers ad cast herself upon the ground in prayer. She really was quite tired but that did not stop her. In her prayers, all of Telbyrin went up to the Creator. But in her fervency, sleep finally fell upon her soul.

ツ ツ ツ ツ ツ ツ

There was a sharp knock at the door. Larilyn awoke.

"My lady!" It was Iomil's voice.

Larilyn stirred from the covers. She had slept quite a long time.

"Come in, Iomil."

The Elf woman darted in.

"The infantry has returned to the gates! May I help tend to them? Oandor may be among them!"

"Of course," said Larilyn quickly. "I'm coming with you." She cast on a green cloak and hurried from the chambers with her maidservant.

The two of them ran down the stairs of the parapets and to the main entrance. A member of the Guard stopped Larilyn.

"Dame Larilyn. It is not safe for you to be out of the palace."

Larilyn ran past him.

"Don't worry," she said. "I'm going to help the soldiers."

The Guardsman ran up to her.

"I cannot let you out, Dame Larilyn," he said. "The king will hold me responsible if anything happens to you."

She grabbed him by the forearms.

"These men need help," she said. "If you wish to attend to my safety then help me with these men."

The Guardsman reluctantly nodded.

Caltirion's physicians came out by the number to tend to the wounded. The uninjured were put to work helping them. Iomil and Larilyn were among them.

"Where is he?" asked Iomil frantically.

"We will find him," said Larilyn trying to console her. A faint voice came from the distance.

"Iomil!"

She turned her head and ran in that direction.

"Oandor, Oandor!" She found him on a stretcher with a physician already tending his leg wound.

"Iomil!" he said. She grabbed his hand.

"I'm here, love," she cried.

Larilyn looked to the infantrymen surrounding them.

"Bring this soldier up to my quarters," she ordered. "He and Iomil and this physician."

"At once, my lady," said the nearest soldier. Two men accompanied by the physician went up to Dame Larilyn's quarters. She and Iomil followed closely behind. When they reached the quarters, Larilyn ordered the doors be opened and led them to a couch. There they placed Oandor's stretcher.

"It's going to be okay, love," cried Iomil.

Larilyn looked to the physician.

"Is he going to be okay?" she asked. The physician was a Human woman, about middle-aged. She looked to the Elf.

"I believe so. He is hearty and should heal fine. It will take some time though before he walks sufficiently.

Iomil looked to her.

"I am a novice physician," she said. "Allow me to help."

The physician nodded. Larilyn looked back to her.

"What is your name, mistress?"

"Enoa, my lady."

Larilyn nodded.

"Thank you for your help, Enoa."

The physician nodded and went to work.

"Iomil," she said. "Get me an herb box and some hot water. I will make a mixture and a tea for him to take away fever and infection." Iomil knew what she was talking about. The Elf leapt up and went to do the physician's bidding. Oandor stirred. His fever was getting worse.

141

"My lady," he said to Larilyn.

Larilyn looked to him.

"Yes, Oandor."

The Elf smiled.

"Your husband is just fine," he said. "He wanted me to tell you that he is fine. He remains in Gallinthrar to defend it from another attack, but he is okay."

Larilyn wiped some tears away from her eyes.

"Thank you, Oandor."

The Elf warrior smiled and slipped out of consciousness.

"Oandor!" said Larilyn.

Enoa put a hand on her shoulder.

"His fever is getting worse, Dame Larilyn. But he is still alive."

Iomil hastened back to the chambers with the requested items. The physician went to work making the laver and tea she had talked about.

"Is he okay?" asked Iomil frantically.

Enoa looked to her.

"He is unconscious from the fever. He should be fine, though. We will pour the laver in the wound, though. It will make it clean. When he re-awakens you can give him the tea."

After they had given Oandor the laver, Commander Lardin walked in.

"Dame Larilyn," he said. "May I speak with you?"

Larilyn looked to the door.

"Yes," she said. She then looked back to Iomil and Enoa.

"I will return," she said, as she and Lardin walked out of the chamber.

"My lady, I have good news and bad news."

"Start with the good," she replied.

"Your husband is in good health," he said. "I swore to him that I would tell you for him. He says he comes for you when the attack on Gallinthrar is all over."

Larilyn nodded.

"Thank you, Commander," she said. "Oandor informed me as well. What is the bad news?"

Lardin sighed.

"A host of Meldron troops approaches Caltirion. My lady, if your husband does not return soon enough I … I don't know what …"

"Relax, Commander," she said. "My husband will come for me. Of that I have no doubt. But what of the people of Caltirion?"

"Caltirion should have a substantial force to hold the city, my lady," he replied. "They will come with their sorcery though; of that I have fear of and my men have no defense from."

Larilyn thought.

"Where is His Reverence?" she asked.

Lardin looked at her curiously.

"Perhaps in the Sanctuary?"

"Hurry there," said Larilyn. "The piece of the Flame which Raltaron brought can ward off sorcery, of that my husband has told me."

Lardin nodded.

"At once, my lady," Lardin said. "You have grown much from a common farm girl, Dame Larilyn. Never let anyone tell you otherwise."

The Commander quickly ran off to the Sanctuary while a cowled figure came up to her. Lardin bowed to him as he ran off. The figure removed his cowl. It was Elrad.

"My lady," he said.

Larilyn smiled and came up to him.

"Yes, Elrad."

The Vicar had a look of utmost seriousness.

"His Reverence is returning to Al-Nartha. I go to the Airells to summon the Elven host to aid us."

"But it is such a long way," said Larilyn. "Does his Majesty know about this?"

"No," replied Elrad. "He needs their help though. Believe me, my lady, we need all the help we can get, especially from the Elves. The Meldron come in great number. My only fear is that when the Elven army arrives, it will be too late."

"Commander Lardin says the defenses will hold," said Larilyn. Elrad looked dismal.

"Not against Meldron sorcery."

"What about the Flame?" she asked.

"The Flame is going out, my lady. Even as we speak it is growing low in the Sanctuary."

"What about Raltaron?" asked Larilyn.

Elrad sighed.

"He also rides to Al-Nartha with the Arch Vicar. The remaining Vicars will tend to Caltirion while I am gone. You must stick to these chambers. And pray that the defenses hold. I doubt that the Airell Elves will reach us in time."

Larilyn nodded.

"I understand."

Elrad sighed and gave her a blessing.

"When Orilin returns," he said. "You must tell him that I will be back."

"I will," said Larilyn. She and Elrad embraced and he took his leave.

When Larilyn returned from her conversations she found Oandor awake and his head in Iomil's lap. She was slowly giving him the tea to drink.

"He is awake," Iomil exclaimed.

Larilyn smiled.

"I see that."

Enoa looked to her.

"He will heal fine, I believe," she said. "My lady, with your leave, I would like to go help tend some others."

"Of course," said Larilyn.

ᔑᔑᔑᔑᔑᔑ

It was a couple of days later and Oandor was able to walk around on crutches. His healing was taking place fast. He continued to stay in Larilyn's chambers while Iomil lived and slept there as well. Larilyn again was sitting out on the balcony watching for her beloved to return. She was worried about so many people, including her maidservant and Oandor. She walked back in to find Iomil giving him more tea.

"Iomil," said Larilyn.

"Yes, my lady."

"I need to speak with you and Oandor about something. Something important. Listen, there is danger approaching the city. I need you and Oandor to ride out toward the Airells. There you will go to the Enclave where Elrad is going. Take shelter in the Enclave."

"My lady!" exclaimed Iomil. "I would not dare think of forsaking you or your lord. I and Oandor will do our part."

"Yes," said Oandor. "I cannot just leave when Caltirion is in need."

Larilyn shook her head.

"You cannot do anything, Oandor. You need to heal. I will see you two alive. Alive, I mean it! I want to see you two live a happy life together. I cannot lose any more friends. I will stay here and wait for Orilin."

"What then, my lady?" asked Iomil.

"I have told him before," she said, "I go where he goes."

"My lady," said Iomil. "We do not wish to do this."

"Then I have to order you then," said Larilyn. "Will you not obey your Dame?"

Iomil hesitated.

"I …"

"Iomil," pleaded Larilyn. "Go. I order this."

Iomil swallowed hard.

"What if your lord does not return? What then, my lady?"

Larilyn grabbed her shoulders.

"He will return," she said. "But I will see you out of the city by nightfall. Will you obey?"

Iomil breathed deeply.

"I will, my lady."

"Good," said Larilyn. "Go to the royal stables and tell the groom to provide you with a small cart and a packhorse.

I will give you supplies for the journey. I know this is asking much, but I will see you two alive. You have better chance of traveling to the Airells than you do here."

Iomil dropped her head and nodded.

"Yes, my lady. I …"

"What is it?" asked Larilyn.

"May I … tell my lady goodbye then?"

"What do you mean?" asked Larilyn. "Of course."

Iomil embraced her. Larilyn smiled and embraced her back.

"I will pray that you and Oandor will live to see happier days. I am not banishing you. I am protecting you. Understand?"

Iomil nodded.

"I will go and gather some things then," said Larilyn.

Larilyn spent the rest of the day gathering supplies for Iomil and Oandor. She felt terrible sending them out like this. Oandor still had a disabled leg, but Larilyn wanted them to take their chances on the road rather than in a besieged city. The way Elrad was speaking about the Meldron sorcery, it sounded dire. Larilyn went down to the royal stables that night and found Oandor and Iomil seated on the cart with the packhorse. Larilyn placed the supplies in the cart.

"Go with all speed," said Larilyn. "The Creator protect you both."

Iomil looked at her.

"May my lord return to my lady and may your days be blessed. I believe we will see each other again, my lady."

"And I," said Larilyn. "Now go."

With that, Iomil and Oandor rode out into the night.

Chapter 16

ANOTHER TWO DAYS PASSED. LARILYN STOOD OUT ON the east parapet with Commander Lardin. A storm rose in the distance.

"They will be here within hours, my lady," said Lardin. The whole army of Caltirion was assembled within the confines of the city. Infantry, cavalry and siege engines were ready to defend. The Lorinthian Guard was stationed at varied positions around the city and there was a host of them around the palace.

"Who leads them I wonder?" asked Larilyn. "A sorcerer?"

"Perhaps," said Lardin. "But we will be ready nonetheless. Commander Gila, Commander of Caltirion's forces, will see to that." They watched the coming storm for a few more minutes before Lardin broke the silence.

"I must be going to join my men, Dame Larilyn."
She looked to him.
"The Creator be with you, Commander."
He saluted and went off.

ϒϒϒϒϒϒ

Umbra Lakar went among the Meldron ranks in front of the city. Her two men-at-arms looked to her.

"Come upon the city with full force," she said. "I will strike at the heart of the forces with the lightning; then they should route in fear. When we breach the city, I will find Lyrinias. The Master is close to dealing with those in Al-Nartha. Soon the Divine Secret will be revealed."

The men-at-arms nodded and started to command orders.

$$\Upsilon \; \Upsilon \; \Upsilon \; \Upsilon \; \Upsilon \; \Upsilon$$

Commanders Aldanar and Lardin watched as the approaching horde advanced; their silver armor gleaming in the distance. With each flash of lightning, more and more were revealed.

"Are they in range of our siege engines?" asked Lardin.

"Just about," replied Aldanar. "A couple more minutes and we will unleash it upon them."

Lardin nodded.

The Meldron advanced a bit more and stopped; their spears high. Umbra came out from among them.

"I offer the men of Caltirion a truce," she yelled. "The time of the Flame is over. The time of the Eternal Secret is now. I am willing to extend mercy if you will submit to it. Hand over your Vicars to us now and you will be spared, all of you. If not, you can be sure this night that we will spare no one.

"Let me through!" yelled Aldanar. He made his way through the ranks and up to the gate.

"Open the gate!" he yelled. The two guards looked at him quizzically.

"My lord?' they replied.

"Open the gates!" he shouted again. The gates were opened and Aldanar strode out fully armed. He went out a stone's throw from Umbra.

"Umbra Lakar!" he yelled. "You have deceived us! I take it you broke off from Barras Drin?" Umbra stared at him with her piercing yellow eyes.

"Naturally!" she said.

"And you want us to just hand over the Vicars to you as if they were cattle?"

"Indeed," she replied.

Aldanar lifted his shield and placed the spear on top of it in the groove. It started to rain.

"We will never do such a thing. You may have disturbed the Flame, but you will not disturb our Vicars. I challenge you to single combat. If I defeat you, your army will leave this place at once."

Umbra stared at him.

"You would be most wise to take that back, Aldanar."

Aldanar readied his spear again.

"I have taken an oath to the death for Her Majesty. Accept my offer and let only our blood be spilt tonight."

"Aldanar!" yelled Commander Lardin. He frantically went among his sergeants.

"Someone has to stop him!" he said.

Umbra smiled at Aldanar.

"And if I defeat you?"

Aldanar smiled.

"Then there would be no avoiding you laying siege to the city, but we will never just hand the Vicars over to you."

Umbra nodded.

"Understood, Captain."

Aldanar smiled.

"I'm not Captain anymore, Umbra. The Little Hawk is here. And you will not defeat him!"

"Aldanar, no!" yelled Lardin.

Umbra's eyes widened.

"Little Hawk?" she said smiling. "My Aldanar, I don't know what is worse; your valor or your tongue." She leaped forward ten feet with sword drawn and crashed into Aldanar's shield splintering his spear. Aldanar drew back and drew his sword. The two fought fiercely. Umbra's strikes with her sword were lightning fast. Aldanar, for all his skill, was having trouble deflecting them. He responded with swift strokes of his own. The battle raged for several minutes. Lardin looked and ran around frantically, but he could not interfere for fear of the Meldron army retaliating.

Aldanar tried to bash his shield into Umbra's side but she rolled and dodged it. She came up and sliced through Aldanar's breastplate and kicked him five feet across the way. He fell and then tried to get up reaching for his sword.

Umbra paced around him as he lay on the ground.

"You may have it," she chided. Aldanar grabbed his side, the blood seeping from between his fingers.

"I'm not done with you yet," he said as he grabbed his sword and got up.

Umbra smirked.

"Yes you are, Aldanar. You were from the beginning. I'm merely toying with you."

Lightning then spouted from her fingers on her left hand and the force of the shock blew Aldanar back against the battlement walls of the city. He tried to get up despite the swoon that was coming upon him. Umbra went over to him.

"You were foolish, Aldanar, for not taking back that threat!" she smiled. She then swiftly impaled him with her sword and he died there beneath the walls of Caltirion.

"Aldanar!" yelled Lardin. Commander Gila stood next to him.

"Ready your men!" he said gruffly. He then gave the signal to the men on the siege works.

"Fire!" he screamed. The siege engines shot hot flaming balls of fire and pitch upon the Meldron, and many of them died on the spot.

"Fire!" yelled Umbra to her men. The Meldron responded with a volley of arrows at Caltirion's battlements and their own siege engines fired. Flaming balls pounded upon the parapets. Caltirion responded with volley after volley of arrows.

Commander Gila ran down to the ranks of the Guard as the battle was raging. There he found young Marin Kar; a formidable Human warrior who was deadly with the spear.

"Aldanar is dead, and Orilin is not here," he said to Marin. "Take command of the Guard."

Marin looked at him reluctantly and saluted.

"What is your command, Commander?" he asked.

Gila gritted his teeth.

"Guard the gates. Let none of them pass. And if they try, let them feel your spears!"

Marin nodded and gave the command for the Guard to regroup and defend the gates.

The battle raged on. Men of Caltirion fell from the parapets to their death by arrows and more Meldron were mowed down by fiery balls from siege engines. The Meldron raised their shields and ran up with the battering ram. The ram gave a blow upon the gates. Arrows were fired down upon them but they were deflected by the shields.

"We can't keep this up all night, Lardin!" yelled Gila. "Tell your men to assemble and …"

Suddenly Umbra Lakar was upon them. She had mounted one of the towers, jumped into the midst of a group of men and mowed them down by sword and lightning. Several of the men screamed and ran, but were blown away by further lightning.

"You have to get to safety now!" yelled Lardin to Commander Gila. He then looked to two infantrymen.

"Guide the Commander to the center battlements!"

They obeyed and led Gila swiftly away.

A group of about twelve men attacked Umbra at once. Three were killed swiftly by the sword. The others attacked her, but she deflected their blows, back-flipped and spouted more lightning, blowing two others off the parapets. The rest attacked but she dodged by jumping to the top of a tower. The archers in the tower were all killed by her sword. Then she took a bow and rained arrows down on unsuspecting men.

"Get away from there!" yelled Lardin.

The men did so.

"Regroup on the south parapet. Those men need

reenforcements!"

Marin Kar hefted a spear through a Meldron who wielded the battering ram. More archers rained down arrows on the battering ram and killed Meldron troops.

"Send fire arrows on that thing!" yelled Commander Lardin from the top. The archers did so. The Meldron had to leave the battering ram. The Guard was unleashed through the gates and sheared through Meldron troops. They put up their shields and the Caltirion archers responded by a hail of arrows into the Meldron ranks. The Guard kept pounding away at the enemy, retreated and the gate was shut.

Umbra ran out of arrows and jumped from the tower and unleashed a scything of pure death upon her enemies. Many men died there.

"Marin!" yelled Lardin. "My men need help! Stop that sorceress!" Marin and ten of the Guard ran up to the north parapet and tried to aid Lardin's men. Marin flew a spear at Umbra with all his might. She dodged, but it grazed her on her left thigh. She screamed and jumped at the Guardsmen. The fight was very hard. Only two Guardsmen were wounded. She then, clearly outnumbered, jumped from amidst them and off to the west.

"Where is she going?" asked one of the Guard.

"She is going to the Sanctuary," said Marin. "Follow me!" The Guard ran toward the Sanctuary trying to find Umbra as best they could. But she was nowhere to be found.

The Meldron sent another barrage of fireballs upon the city walls. Caltirion's archers were running out of fire arrows. Captain Nidor of the cavalry sounded for his troops to make for the back gate. Commander Lardin made his way among his men.

"Infantry! Regroup!"

The first ranks of Caltirion's infantry made ready and then were unleashed through the gates.

"Crush them!" yelled Lardin. "Push them forward!"

Nidor was almost to the south gates when he sounded his battle horn.

"Men! Let us go to Lardin's aid. Attack them from the

south and route their ranks!"

The cavalry were unleashed through the south gates and made the charge toward the Meldron ranks. The charge distracted them so that the Caltirion infantry crushed them back. Meldron archers responded to the cavalry charge and several horsemen fell.

"Break them!" yelled Nidor.

The cavalry soon bashed into the Meldron forces with full force. The forces were sandwiched in between infantry and cavalry and it seemed as if they were going to route. Then a Meldron trumpet sounded. Nidor looked up in horror at what he saw. It was their cavalry upon the Nesdarath: the black horses of the Meldron who were raised in the darkness and knew only their masters. The Nesdarath were trained to be without fear and came armored.

Another trumpet sounded. Three Meldron sorcerers came forward and unleashed fire upon Caltirion's cavalry. Many men died in the blast, and the forces routed.

"Fall back!" yelled Nidor. "Fall back! Lardin, get out of there!"

The Commander of the infantry heeded and commanded his forces to fall back. Another blast of fire was unbridled upon Nidor's forces. The Nesdarath were now upon them also. Nidor and his men ran with all their might while the Nesdarath brigade cut them down. Their commander came in a war chariot and yielded a deadly bow. Four Nesdarath pulled the chariot. No one was able to withstand him.

"Through the gates!" yelled Nidor.

But it was a critical error. The Nesdarath broke the Caltirion ranks and some were able to enter the city. They mowed down all in their path. Nidor signaled for his men to retreat west. Some of the Nesdarath pursued, but most charged into the city. Caltirion's archers were there to meet them, and several of the enemy went down in a shower of arrows.

"Fire!" yelled the Captain of the archers. "Drive them back!" More and more of the Meldron horsemen dropped from Caltirion arrows. Two units of Caltirion infantry digressed from the east and went to meet the dreaded Meldron cavalry. Marin Kar and his men also heard of the calamity.

"One unit defend the east!" he barked. "The next unit come with me." Meldron siege engines fired. The state of Caltirion's forces were now put in a panic.

$$\Upsilon \; \Upsilon \; \Upsilon \; \Upsilon \; \Upsilon \; \Upsilon$$

Larilyn stood upon the palace battlements watching the fire within the city and the siege engines firing. Two Guardsmen approached her.

"Dame Larilyn," they said. "We must bring you into the inner palace where you can be put to safety." Larilyn looked back at them.

"What about all the other women and children of the city?!"

The Guardsmen nodded.

"We are working on that. Come with us, my lady." Larilyn reluctantly obeyed and went with them through a corridor down some stairs lit with sconces. They then led her out through a short, paved courtyard that led into the inner palace. There King Lyrinias, in his armor, was waiting for her.

"My lady," he said. "We have been most worried about you. You must come and join the queen and the rest inside."

Larilyn looked at him.

"My liege," she said. "There are women and children out there. Can we send the Guard to gather them?"

"Lardin's forces should be looking after that," said Lyrinias. "I am about to go myself to join the Guard."

"My liege," said Larilyn. "Won't you be putting yourself in danger?"

The king laughed a bit.

"Such are the ways of war, my lady. Come, I will see you safe and sound."

They came into the inner palace and into the throne room. The gate was shut behind them. What Larilyn saw

horrified her. There, standing next to the queen, was the
Meldron sorceress she had seen in the Dreath Wood. It was
Umbra Lakar. She had her sword drawn and eyed Larilyn.
The Guard around the throne stood at attention but the Guard
around Larilyn backed up and drew their swords. Larilyn
looked to the king.

"What is this, my liege?!"

The king looked to her and then to Umbra.

"Do what you will, Umbra," he said. The Guard who
stood by the queen descended and grabbed Larilyn by the
arms.

"Liar!" yelled Larilyn to the king. "You're not going into
battle!"

Lyrinias smiled.

"You're right, my lady. What lay hidden from all time
lays before me." He paced around.

"Ha!" he laughed. "Do you honestly think I could pass
up the opportunity to learn what has lain hidden since the
beginning of the world?"

"What in the world are you talking about?!" yelled
Larilyn. "You allowed a Meldron sorceress into your throne
room!"

"Only a teacher," said Lyrinias. "One who will guide
us all."

"To what?!" shouted Larilyn.

"To the Divine Secret," said Lyrinias. "Don't you get
it, Larilyn? We don't need the Flame anymore. Ralharin's
prophecy is coming to pass. The Flame will be snuffed out
and the Vicars will be put to route. And now the Divine Secret
will be revealed. This will be the true gift of the Creator. Not
what the petty Vicars like to tell us."

"I don't need this secret!" yelled Larilyn. "When my
husband gets here, he will deal with you."

"Oh yes," said Umbra. "We want him indeed."

Larilyn eyed the Meldron woman fiercely.

"Don't come near me, you witch!"

Umbra laughed.

"You don't know the beginning of that word, farm girl,"

she scoffed. The Guardsmen next to Larilyn drew near to Umbra. One of them spoke up.

"I cannot accept your judgment on this, my liege. We were ordered to protect Dame Larilyn."

"You are the Queen's Guard!" snarled Lyrinias. "You will do as you are told!"

"We will see Dame Larilyn safe, my liege," said the Guardsman.

"Umbra," said Lyrinias casually. Umbra unexpectedly attacked the Guardsman and killed him where he stood. The other Guardsman attacked her. The battle was fierce but brief, and he was killed there.

"Would any more Guardsmen like to betray his or her Majesty?" yelled Lyrinias. "No? Very well. Umbra, do as you wish."

The Meldron woman went over to Larilyn and slapped her across the face with the back of her hand. Larilyn went down to the ground. She crawled over to a dead Guardsman's sword and reached for it. Umbra walked over to her, kicked it out of the way, kicked Larilyn in the stomach and put her blade up to her throat. The breath was knocked out of Larilyn and she heaved for air.

"I need you alive," said Umbra. "I don't really care about you, though – I care about him."

"Who?" breathed Larilyn.

"Why, the Little Hawk, my dear."

Larilyn looked up at her in anger.

"When he gets here … he will … he …"

"Ha!" laughed Umbra. She kicked Larilyn again.

Larilyn gazed up at the queen.

"Your … Majesty," she heaved. "Do … something."

"I cannot, Larilyn."

Larilyn gazed up at her in wonder.

"What?"

"You were a tool, 'Dame' Larilyn," she chided. "And you're a tool to get your husband killed."

"How … can you allow this?" asked Larilyn.

"I am Queen, my dear," said Lirana.

Larilyn glared at her.

"And I am a lady of the realm!"

"You are a tool for your husband's death and nothing more," said Lirana. "Besides, your life has no more meaning. You are only a meager farm girl; a dry vine who cannot even bear children. Your parents were murdered by the Meldron and when we get through with your husband, you will be theirs."

Larilyn was deeply hurt by the queen's words and tears started to well up in her eyes.

"Orilin will come for me!" she cried.

Umbra laughed at her.

"That's the plan," she said.

Larilyn gazed up at her and then to the queen.

"If you wanted him, why did you order him out of Caltirion?"

Umbra shook her head and laughed.

"We wanted to lead him to his death with the Menetarrans, but since we have reports that he is still alive, I will deal with him. Either way, he will die. He thought he was being a hero wielding the Malanthar. He is only a tool like you. A piece on the board that needed to be removed from here."

"I could not just order his death," replied Lyrinias. "I myself would have been killed by my own people for killing a hero of Telbyrin. But if he was killed in battle, then it would look perfectly natural."

"He is now the piece that needs to be taken out to bring a crushing defeat of morale among Caltirion!" said Umbra. "Can you imagine what that will do to them when the warrior who wielded the Malanthar is dead!? The lasting hope of the Flame will be snuffed out!"

Larilyn glared at them.

"May the curse of Cyrus be upon you all!" she screamed.

Umbra laughed.

"Take her away," she said.

Two Guardsmen did so. Umbra looked back at a page boy. She jumped over to him with lightning speed and pointed her sword up to his throat.

"Please," he begged. "Don't kill me!"

Umbra smiled at him.

"If you obey the next order, I will not kill you. Ride to Gallinthrar and find Orilin Alandiron. When you find him tell him that Dame Larilyn is captured and is being held by me. If you do not deliver this message or Orilin Alandiron does not come, I will slit you from top to bottom. Understand?"

"Yes," groaned the boy.

"Off with you now," said Umbra. The page boy left the throne room in a fierce run. Umbra turned back to the king.

"Orilin Alandiron is now our fish for the trap!"

Chapter 17

WHEN ELRAD ENTERED THE GATES OF THE AIRELL Enclave it was early evening. The western sun created orange and pink colors in the clouds high above the snowy mountains. There was no war here, no battle alarm; only peace. Elrad sighed to himself as he thought of this. How guilty he felt for bringing this tragic war to these peaceful Elves who only wanted to start an Elven civilization over after the tragedy of Laerdiron. The guardsmen stood at the gate.

"Is your visit peaceful, Elrad?"

He looked up.

"Unfortunately not," he said. "I bring ill news from Caltirion."

The guardsmen nodded and let him in. He was led inside a city filled with his people. They were going about life as usual: peaceful. The river ran past the Elven town and carried its glacial water towards the east. Green cyprus and cedar grew around the town and a forest of the former was toward the south. Small farms scattered the Airell valley and the goods were brought to the town daily. This town the Elves left unnamed. They hoped with all their hearts that it would become the next Laerdiron.

Elrad was led past a couple of Elven women carrying apples in baskets. They bowed politely to him as they passed.

"Our people here have no idea what is going on, do they?" asked Elrad to the guard.

"About the Flame, as you know, we do," he said. "What is the cause behind it?"

Elrad sighed a bit.

"It has to do with the tidings I bring today. In the east a war is raging." The guard looked back.

"Between whom?"

Elrad looked ahead.

"I will tell Armid when I see him, and you."

The guard nodded and continued on.

Elrad continued on his way down the cobbled streets past a farrier and a general store. More houses and chalets lay nestled around the streets and up into the hills. The city was, of course, covered by a vast wall with four guard towers. Elrad made his way up a steep street leading up a hill on top of which lay a vast alpine stronghold. It was built of cedar and the top of it was highly pointed. On the front part of the roof stood a statue of a ram's head. The roof was lightly covered with a bit of snow. Two armored guards stood watch, and when they saw Elrad they let him pass.

The guards led him into the great hall where sat the Elven overseer and his wife. There was another Elven couple seated around them. The overseer had black hair cropped short and wore a dark blue and white robe. His wife had blond tresses and wore a green gown. When they saw Elrad, they both rose.

"Welcome Elrad," said the overseer. "We have been greatly expecting someone to give us word on Raltaron."

"Thank you, Armid," replied Elrad bowing his head. "And you Hithena, you are looking well."

Armid's wife bowed a little.

"Very well, lord Vicar." The couple next to them got up.

"Thank you, as well, for receiving me," said Elrad. "What are your names?"

"Dalvin and Tali, lord Vicar," they said.

Elrad bowed his head.

"Allow me to get to the matter at hand, my lord Armid, for there is no time to waste. You asked of Raltaron. He has gone to Al-Nartha. His Reverence has also gone. The Flame was brought to Caltirion by Raltaron as you know but now has gone out. This situation has grown more dire than imagined. Caltirion is under siege. Under siege, that is, by Meldron troops. The Menetarrans have struck from the south at Gallinthrar. My adopted son, Orilin, has been deployed with the Lorinthian Guard to aid it. I have no doubt that he will be successful, but Caltirion still needs great aid. To be honest, I hate to come to you with such calamitous news – especially when our people are trying to rebuild our civilization."

"Who is behind all of this, Elrad?" asked Armid

"I'm not entirely sure, my lord," he replied. "His Majesty does not even know that I'm here. I came in secret because I feared he would have refused me. Whether he likes it or not, he needs our help."

Armid narrowed his gaze.

"What do you propose that we do?"

"Deploy the Elven army, my lord," said Elrad. "We have no threat here in the Airells to worry about."

"Raltaron was our Vicar," said Armid. "If we deploy, will you lead us as Vicar?"

"I will," replied Elrad. "Though his Majesty will probably dispense me from his service. But it is a price that I am willing to pay if it means stability in the world once again. This city is perhaps one of the only places left in the world that houses the Flame besides Al-Nartha. With that we will be able to fight off the Meldron sorcery."

"You mentioned your son, Elrad," said Armid. "Do you believe that he is well?"

Elrad smiled.

"If I know anything about Orilin it is that he will be well. Armid, he wields the Malanthar."

The Elves looked to each other.

"I thought only a king could wield that blade," replied Hithena.

"The king has given leave over to Orilin for that," said Elrad. "Orilin is now Captain of the Guard and the king's champion."

Armid arose from his chair and paced.

"Has Orilin helped to secure Gallinthrar?"

Elrad nodded.

"I can only believe that he has, my lord. My estimates say that the Menetarran hordes do not have the strength to overpower both Gallinthrar and Caltirion's forces. Besides, Orilin would not have left the city until it was secure."

Armid kept pacing.

"And we do not know why the Meldron are attacking? Can it have something to do with their Divine Secret or prophecies?"

Elrad gazed at him.

"The more I've thought of it the more I believe that to be the case, although I still do not know who is behind all of this. Orilin has told me that Barras Drin's forces are heading towards the south. I can only suppose it to be Al-Nartha. Last I heard, they are accompanied by a Meldron sorceress."

Armid shot a gaze of uneasiness at the Vicar.

"Tell me more."

Elrad cleared his throat and continued.

"Orilin and his wife, Larilyn, came to us from Sargna where they discovered that the Flame was out. To seek refuge from Barras Drin, they hid in the Dreath Wood. They barely escaped notice. It was then that they saw the Meldron sorceress. Lyrinias knows of her too. The Elven scouts from Caltirion have discovered that she is named Umbra Lakar."

Armid looked toward Elrad.

"She must be a new addition. I have not heard of her before."

Elrad nodded.

"She is, my lord."

"And she rides with Barras Drin toward the south?"

"The last I heard of it, that was the case, my lord."

Armid sighed.

"The Meldron are devious. When I studied under Kal-Ardaan, when we learned of the Battle of Rak Mardan, it was he who told us of discovering weaknesses in the Meldron's plans. It was only then that the Elves routed them with the Malanthar and our armies. In other words, lord Vicar, you can have a great force, but you have to know the loopholes in their plans. In a word, be ready for anything."

"That is why we need the Airell army, my lord," said Elrad. "Caltirion is not as skilled in fighting the Meldron as we are."

Armid nodded.

"There is another matter, Elrad," he continued. "You and I both studied under Kal-Ardaan so you will know this. It is from the Chronicles of Laerdiron. When Cyrus and Ralharin did battle, Cyrus defeated him. And Ralharin mentioned an "eternal antipathy" between his race and ours. Cyrus, as you know, cursed their race. After Ralharin was burned by the Flame, he stated that the Flame would be snuffed out and the Vicars would be put to route. He also stated that 'he' would never forgive nor forget."

Elrad nodded.

"That is not the modern translation, my lord. The translation says that 'my race' will never forgive nor forget."

"Ah, yes," said Armid. "But you know nevertheless the old translations."

Elrad nodded.

"I do, my lord. Many scholars have changed Ralharin's 'I' to encompass the whole race."

"And there lies their error," said Armid.

"Why are translations so important at this time?" remarked Elrad. "With all due respect, my lord, now is not the time for scholarship. Now is the time for war. Ralharin is dead. We have much else to be concerned about."

"There is another possible error."

Elrad gasped a bit and then paced. He thought hard.

"You are surely not referring to the Dark Resurgence?"

Armid nodded gravely.

"I am."

Elrad gazed at the Elf lord and then paced about again.

"I myself have doubted it for some time," remarked Armid. "It's an old theory but one that was dreaded nevertheless. The Flame has continued to go out over all the world, but with the Elves it still burns. I can only assume that it still burns in Al-Nartha. If Ralharin is resurrected, then there will be no one to stop him. All, save one. This battle lies in Al-Nartha, not in Caltirion."

"I have never believed that the Meldron had the power to raise the dead," said Elrad. "Although some believe this, including his Reverence."

"The Meldron perhaps want you not to believe it, lord Vicar," remarked Armid. "I will deploy the Elven army to Caltirion with you to lead us, but when, and if, we defeat the Meldron, we need to continue to Al-Nartha."

Elrad looked in wonder.

"Won't the forces of the south be enough to hold off Barras Drin? Raltaron and his Reverence ride to the Sacred Temple. They will be enough to calm the people."

Armid chuckled a bit.

"Elrad, for such a renowned, wise Vicar you are being duped. The Dark Resurgence is upon us. I especially believe this now after your current tidings."

"Lord Armid!" exclaimed Elrad. "You are speaking of the continuation of a primordial battle! The Dark Resurgence not only involves the resurrection of Ralharin but will involve two individuals: one who is dead and one whom we have no knowledge of if he has Faded. That is what the ancient prophecies tell us about it. Those prophecies have no solid ground anyway. And there is no evidence that the Patriarch is still among us. If he is, wouldn't he still be with our people? He most surely has Faded by now."

Armid smiled a little and looked the Vicar in the eyes solemnly.

"He has indeed not, Elrad. Come, I will tell you more."

Chapter 18

Taelin rode his horse into Gallinthrar's gates. His horse was almost dead of exhaustion and the guardsmen inside the gates immediately began to tend to her.

"Where is Captain Orilin?!" exclaimed Taelin. "I need to find him as fast as I can."

The guardsmen looked to each other.

"Is there some sort of trouble, boy?" they asked.

"Please," said Taelin. "I don't have time to explain. I need to find Captain Orilin."

One of the guards nodded.

"I will take you to him. He is up on the battlements with the rest of the Guard."

As the two were walking up to the battlements the guard lay a hand on Taelin's shoulder.

"We have routed the Menetarrans."

Taelin looked up at him.

"Thank the Creator! There remains much to be done though. The Meldron hosts are not so easily routed."

The guard looked to him.

"We will do what we can." The two reached the top of the battlements and Captain Orilin stood among the Guard with Captain Hadix talking. Taelin ran up to him.

"Captain Orilin!" he exclaimed. "Captain!"

Orilin looked over to the boy who was perspiring and had a wild look in his eyes.

Hadix piped up.

"Get away, boy! Can't you see that Captain Orilin is busy?"

Taelin ignored the huge man and pushed his way through.

"Captain Orilin!"

"Let him through," said Orilin.

The men parted a way for Taelin to get through.

"What is it, lad? Who are you?" he continued.

"Taelin, my lord," he said. "I am page to his Majesty."

A commotion arose among the men.

"Go on," said Orilin. "Is his Majesty in some sort of trouble?"

Taelin swallowed hard. His breathing rate increased.

"It's okay," said Orilin. "What is it?"

Taelin closed his eyes and took a deep breath.

"Umbra Lakar has breached the palace."

A huge commotion arose among the men then.

"Quiet!" yelled Hadix. "Quiet! Let the boy speak!"

Taelin continued.

"His Reverence has left Caltirion for who knows where. What is more, his Majesty has sided with the sorceress. He has sided with the Meldron!"

Orilin's eyes went wide. He grabbed Taelin by the shoulders.

"What do you mean?!" he exclaimed.

Taelin was very afraid at this point.

"I mean he … he wants … to share in their Divine Secret or something like that. She … she sent me to you, my lord."

"Who?" asked Orilin.

"Umbra Lakar. She … she has captive the Dame Larilyn!"

Orilin's eyes went wild. He gritted his teeth and stared the boy in the eye.

"Where have they put her?!"

"I don't know, my lord," said Taelin.

"What did they do to her?!"

"They … they …"

"Yes?!" yelled Orilin. "Go on?!"

"They…they slapped her, my lord," said Taelin with tears in his eyes. "They … they kicked her."

Orilin's breathing increased. His grip on Taelin increased. Suddenly he let go and let out a violent scream.

He drew the Malanthar and struck it against a point on the battlements. Sparks flew and the stone point was cleaved in two. The men were silent. Hadix quickly broke it.

"Captain Orilin."

"Let me be!" he exclaimed. All were silent again. Orilin stood there with the sword and breathed deeply.

"I …" he growled, shaking his head slowly. "I will kill them both for this!"

Taelin worked up his courage.

"Captain Orilin," he said. "She is being held by Umbra Lakar. I have delivered my message, possibly my last."

Orilin shook his head.

"You have done well, Taelin," he said. "I will take it from here."

Hadix walked up to Orilin.

"It's a trap, my lord," he said. "They want you to get yourself killed. You have already threatened his Majesty's life. That in itself is an offense punishable by death. If you go after his Majesty, the Guard will certainly kill you."

Orilin looked around at the rest of the Guard.

"Then why have not the rest of you killed me?" he asked.

The Guard were speechless.

"This boy," continued Orilin. "We know that delivering a message of libel about his Majesty is an offense punishable by death also. Why have you not killed him?"

Taelin looked to Orilin nervously.

"Is it possible that you believe him?" asked Orilin.

A Guardsman stepped up.

"It is, my lord. Besides, we could not kill you without proper evidence. Caltirion has a law. But that is beside the point."

Orilin looked at him and then back to the boy.

Hadix spoke up again.

"Caltirion has a law indeed! Launching or even talking about an attack upon his Majesty's life is high treason. You all are no match for Caltirion's forces by yourselves. You will all die!"

Orilin looked to Hadix.

"Then what do you propose that we do, Commander Hadix?" he bellowed.

"Umbra Lakar has you by the throat, my lord," he said to Orilin. "You cannot just walk into Caltirion, killing as you go, and storm the palace."

"They have my wife!" he exclaimed.

Hadix shook his head.

"It's bait for you. You cannot save her, my lord."

"By the Creator, I can!" shouted Orilin.

Hadix walked up to him.

"What are you going to do, Captain?" he said calmly. "Take these men with you, storm Caltirion's battlements with dozens of archers raining arrows upon you, take on the rest of the Lorinthian Guard who guard the palace, break into the palace, kill a Meldron sorceress and his Majesty, not to mention the rest of the Lorinthian Guard surrounding the throne room and his throne? You are a mighty warrior, Captain, but you would be dead before you breached the gates!"

"You underestimate my men, Commander," growled Orilin.

"I do not," said Hadix. "But right now you are not in your right mind. You are letting these Elven Passions take control of you. Can they not make you Fade?" There was another silence.

"Again, what do you suggest that we do, Commander Hadix?" asked Orilin.

"There is not much you can do right now. But in the end, you must do what is right for Caltirion and, indeed, Telbyrin. You are Captain of the Queen's Guard."

"What do you mean by that?" asked Orilin.

Hadix looked at him intently.

"You have to accept that you may not get your wife back, Captain. They may, indeed, kill her anyway."

"I WILL get her back, Hadix!" growled Orilin.

All were silent again watching Orilin. Taelin spoke up again.

"There is another piece of information, my lord; one that I swear is true. If it is not, then the Guard can kill me here at once."

Orilin looked to the boy.

"You're getting braver by the second, Taelin. What is the news?"

Taelin swallowed.

"The Queen has also joined the King in their rebellion. They seek the Divine Secret of the Meldron. The Guard can no longer fight for a noble queen."

Jinak, a Human Guard, looked to Taelin.

"Very bold words among the Guard, Taelin. Something that could, indeed, get you killed here on the spot. The Guard fights for her Majesty until death."

Orilin looked to Jinak and held up a hand. He then looked back to Taelin.

"How do you know this?"

"I saw it with my own eyes, my lord!" he exclaimed. "I am not lying to you. Take me to Caltirion. If I am lying, you may kill me yourself!"

"Enough about this talk of killing!" said Orilin. "There has been enough blood spilt over these past days."

Taelin nodded.

"The Queen insulted your wife, my lord," he continued. "She called Dame Larilyn a dry vine."

Orilin bowed his head and nodded.

"This boy must have heard it from the Queen's mouth. He would not just know such a thing. My wife certainly would not have told him."

Jinak spoke up.

"What do you mean, Captain?"

Orilin looked up.

"My wife is barren. That is a grief we have been carrying for some time. Again, this boy would not just have known that. He had to have heard it from someone."

Jinak's face grew solemn.

"Why from the Queen's mouth?"

Orilin turned to look at the men.

"I do not believe this boy is lying. He has indeed laid out his life before us. The Vicar Raltaron told me that much more was ahead of me. Besides being a conniving cleric, I have to admit he is one of the wisest I know. I, for one am going to Caltirion to investigate."

"How will you get in, Captain?" asked a young Guard.

"I will be welcome under Commander Lardin's men. Indeed, they will be glad to see us. I don't know what to do about his Majesty yet, but I will find a way to deal with this sorceress. And I will rescue my wife."

There was a silence.

"Will anyone aid me in this?" asked Orilin.

The Guard looked to each other.

"I know your fear and your hesitancy," said Orilin. "You are loyal until death to his and her Majesty. But you are also loyal to your country. If any of you do not feel comfortable with this, then you can leave me and report to his Majesty, if that is what you so wish."

"We could report to his Majesty," said Jinak, "But we would be forsaking our Captain."

Orilin nodded and sighed a bit.

"All of you who will aid me, come over to my side."

Again the Guard hesitated. Jinak and two young Guardsmen crossed over. Others slowly followed until all the Guardsmen were across.

"Sixteen out of the twenty-four of us left, counting myself," said Orilin.

One of the younger Guardsmen, Dirnor, spoke up.

"If Taelin is right, we are men now without any king or queen to fight for. All we have is Caltirion and you, Captain."

Orilin nodded solemnly.

"We go then?"

The Guard responded with their yes.

"We will not attack the citadel," said Orilin. "We will report to commander Lardin. He will most certainly welcome us. Commander Hadix. I take it you will need to tend to Gallinthrar City now?"

Hadix shook his head.

"We have men who can do that. I will leave two companies to help the Vicars and the people tend to those in need. I myself and the rest will go to help secure Caltirion. We need to find out where the Meldron strike."

Taelin spoke up.

"When last I left, my lord, they were still striking the east battlements."

Hadix nodded.

"We need to enter through the quickest route."

Orilin looked to Taelin.

"You said earlier that His Reverence has left the city? You don't know where he went?

"No, my lord."

Orilin looked to his men.

"This poses a bigger problem. When we reach Caltirion, after we make contact with Lardin, we will need to make sure the Vicars are safe."

ᚲᚲᚲᚲᚲᚲ

Raltaron and Hhrin-Calin journeyed to the Sacred City: Al-Nartha. It lay quiet and desolate. Armed men were crowding the walls. They looked to the two as they approached.

"Hhrin-Calin!" one of them yelled.

"Yes!" exclaimed His Reverence. "I am here to see Barras Drin." There were two large bronze gates with an image of the Eternal Flame on it. It slowly opened. The

Arch-Vicar and Raltaron went into the city to see vast numbers of people numbed with fear. Some looked in hope to Hhrin-Calin. One woman came up to him.

"Your Reverence! Thank the Creator you are here! Will you help us?"

"I will do what I can," said Hhrin-Calin.

He and Raltaron were led up the streets to the Sacred Temple by the guard. The temple was square-shaped and walled with bronze. A massive cobbled courtyard lay around it with fountains. On the walls were the different races holding the Flame up to the Creator. In front of the Temple was a mass of men clad in brown and black metal-studded armor. A large man stepped out. He was a tan skinned man in the same type of armor. He had a thin black beard and hair. One eye was glazed over, as it was blinded. The other was dark-colored.

"Barras Drin!" yelled Raltaron. "You have dared to attack the Sacred City? What...?"

Hhrin-Calin raised his hand to Raltaron.

"I will do the speaking, Raltaron," he said.

Raltaron bowed back in reverence.

"What do you mean by attacking this city?" asked Hhrin-Calin.

Barras Drin looked to him.

"I have secured this city for the Great One," he said boldly. Hhrin-Calin's eyebrows raised.

"Do you mean Umbra Lakar?"

"No," said Barras Drin. "He is inside and will speak with you. All I wanted was the gold. I have gotten this and will leave shortly."

"Yes, I would like to see this Great One of yours," said Hhrin-Calin. "I would like to meet the person who would dare plan the rape of this most sacred place. But by right of Arch-Vicar, I and Vicar Raltaron will enter the Temple."

Barras Drin smiled and stepped aside. Hhrin-Calin and Raltaron advanced toward the entrance. As they entered, mosaics of the different races surrounded the ceiling holding the Flame. Mosaics of the history of the world also surrounded them. Gorgeous marbled paths lined the inside. At the center, in a huge bronze and marble table roared the Eternal Flame brightly. This was where it was believed the finger of the Creator first touched Telbyrin. The Flame grew high in the temple. Raltaron smiled.

"It seems not to have dimmed a bit, your Reverence."

Hhrin-Calin turned to him and smiled.

"Yes," he said. The doors were shut behind them. Raltaron looked back. Two cowled figures stepped out from behind the Flame and approached them.

"You are here to see the Great One?" one of them asked.

Hhrin-Calin stepped forward.

"Yes we are!"

There was a moment of silence. Only the burning of the Flame could be heard. Then another cowled figure stepped out of the shadows at the very back of the Temple. He approached them.

"Long have I known that one race was left out of the Eternal Song. But it was indeed of their choosing."

Raltaron looked around in nervousness. The other two figures took off their cowls. They were Meldron.

The other figure walked up closer. Raltaron readied his staff.

"Your Reverence!"

The center figure gestured with his arm and blew back Raltaron with a huge blow. He hit the ground, winced in pain and reached for his staff.

"Your Reverence!" yelled Raltaron. But Hhrin-Calin did nothing. He stood there and watched the figure approach Raltaron.

"An ETERNAL antipathy be between your race and mine, oh Cyrus! Behold, I will never forgive nor forget!"

Raltaron looked up. The figure removed his cowl.

"May the curse I first lay upon you remain, Ralharin!" shouted Raltaron. "This fight is between you and me. Let the people of Al-Nartha go!"

Ralharin laughed.

"This fight has been between me and this idolatrous world, Cyrus."

Hhrin-Calin looked down at Raltaron.

"So you, indeed, are the Patriarch."

"Traitor!" shouted Raltaron. "You are a traitor to your people and to all the Vicars, Hhrin-Calin!"

The Arch Vicar smiled.

"When I was promised to know the Divine Secret, how could I resist? The Dark Resurgence has been fulfilled. All that is left is to sacrifice you and the Flame will be snuffed out."

Raltaron laughed.

"What makes you think that? I have ordained count-less Vicars throughout the eons. They all could pass on the Flame. My death will not stop the Eternal Song."

Ralharin spoke up.

"My mission will not be finished until the Flame is snuffed out and the Vicars are put to death along with you, oh Patriarch! With their death and yours, there will be none to ordain."

Raltaron stood up with his staff.

"Then let us finish this! The Eternal Song will continue even without the Vicars. Yes, I am Cyrus! And I stand before the Flame to glorify the Creator! By my life or by my death, I serve Him. And all of Telbyrin, even if plunged into darkness will die singing the Song forever in the halls of the blessed!"

Chapter 19

ORILIN, THE GUARD AND GALLINTHRAR'S FORCES MADE THEIR way towards the city. They looked out over a large hill to see the east gates of Caltirion in flames. Commander Hadix and Orilin looked out over the hill.

"I and my men need to go through the east gates," said Orilin. "There are too many to the south."

"I have six hundred spears and three hundred cavalry," said Hadix. "The cavalry can create a diversion against those Nesdarath. Caltirion's cavalry were perhaps routed."

Orilin nodded.

"Six hundred spears will hardly be enough to break the Meldron lines."

Hadix looked to him.

"Captain Orilin, the fate of Telbyrin is upon us. If we are to die, we will die defending it."

Orilin nodded again.

"I'll meet up with Lardin. Surely there is more infantry left."

Hadix nodded.

"Then I will create the diversion. But hurry! We will only have so much time to distract those Nesdarath."

Orilin nodded and looked to his men.

"Hurry forth to the east, men. On my lead!"

They readied themselves. Orilin and the Guard strode forth quickly. Hadix was left on the field with his lieutenants. Hadar rode up on his mount.

"Shall I send forth your orders, my lord?"

Hadix nodded.

"Our cavalry will charge head-on into those Nesda-rath. The infantry will charge the Meldron forces to the east from the side. And let us pray that Commander Lardin will have re-enforcements and that the Caltirion cavalry has re-mustered itself." Hadar saluted and went off to rally the men.

ᛉ ᛉ ᛉ ᛉ ᛉ ᛉ

Orilin and his men scattered on his command and entered through the east gates. They were winded from the running. Orilin went up to the nearest guard.

"Captain Orilin!" he exclaimed. "Thank the Creator you are here." Orilin looked to him.

"Take us to Commander Lardin."

The guard saluted.

"Follow me, Captain."

The guard led Orilin and his men throughout the city as fast as he could. It took quite a while. Orilin was careful to avoid close connection with the palace. They reached the east battlements around mid-afternoon.

Commander Lardin stood on the east battlements looking down at wearied men and the wearied Meldron forc-es.

"Captain Orilin!" he shouted. "You are most welcome." Orilin ran up to him.

"How many do you have left?" asked Orilin.

"I'm not sure," he said. "We tried to attack them from around the north gates but they drove us back. It is taking all we are worth to defend them from breaching the city. But they are quite worn out themselves it seems."

Orilin nodded.

"Some of Gallinthrar's forces are here. It's not much but it will be enough to distract those Nesdarath."

Lardin smiled.

"Thank the Creator. That should give us an opportunity to drive them back more."

"There is more dreadful news, Commander. It has been reported that his Majesty has sided with Umbra Lakar."

What?!" exclaimed Lardin. "How?"

"There is a page boy who came to us named Taelin. Here he is. Tell the Commander what you saw."

"He has indeed gone over to their side," said Taelin.

Lardin grimaced.

"That cannot be true. How could that possibly happen?" Taelin came up to him.

"It is true, my lord."

Orilin looked to the Commander.

"They have my wife, Commander. I have to rescue her."

Lardin looked to the Elf and back to the boy.

"How do you know this, boy?" he asked.

"I was there, my lord," replied Taelin. "I swear I saw it. They kicked and slapped Dame Larilyn and took her away to who knows where. Please, my lord, Captain Orilin has to rescue her!"

Lardin looked to Orilin.

"You cannot go charging into the palace, Orilin," he said. "We will have to find another way. Why is the Guard not doing something about this?"

"I don't know," said Orilin. "Perhaps because they have been duped into this themselves."

Lardin looked to him and closed his eyes.

"Marin Kar has taken command over the Guard in the city, Captain. He last went to secure the Sanctuary and to guard it."

"He is a good warrior," said Orilin. "I will not doubt his abilities."

Lardin smiled.

"We must not keep talking here. Captain Orilin, might I suggest that you and your men and head to the Sanctuary? There meet up with Marin. I seriously doubt he has betrayed us." Orilin nodded.

"If he has then that means the end of the Guard and our possible downfall," replied Orilin. "I will go and find him. And let me take this boy with me."

"Very well," said Lardin. "I will look for Commander Hadix's advancements."

Orilin, Taelin, and the Guard made their way through the city toward the Sanctuary. They came across other infantry and Guard patrolling the streets. One of the Guard came up to him.

"Captain Orilin!" he said. "You are back!"

"Yes," he replied. "I need you and the rest of the Guard here to rally with me to the Sanctuary. There let us meet up with Marin Kar."

The Guardsman saluted and joined them.

Orilin gathered about 50 of the Guard to him. As they journeyed toward the Sanctuary, people were crying out after them. One elderly woman came up to them.

"What is the news from the east gates, my lord?" she asked. "Is the city secure?"

"For now," said Orilin. "Stay steady and seek shelter. We are doing everything we can."

The old woman scurried away and joined the group of huddled masses around the buildings. The Guard continued on.

They reached the Sanctuary in the evening. As Orilin walked in it was quiet. A lone acolyte met him. He was a young Elf and his eyes were full on concern.

"Captain Orilin," he said.

Orilin nodded.

"Where are the Vicars?" he asked.

The acolyte looked up.

"They have been summoned to the palace. Only I, Vicar Ulthrel, Marin Kar and his men remain. We are helping to tend and guard the people."

Orilin looked immediately anxious.

"What is your name?"

"Shamil, my lord."

"Shamil," said Orilin. "Take me to your Vicar immediately."

Shamil led the Guard inside the Sanctuary and up to another Elf, young, but obviously more mature than Shamil. He had dark hair much like Orilin's and green eyes.

"I am Ulthrel, my lord," he said.

"Orilin Alandiron," said Orilin. "I will get down to the business at hand. I and my men have to get inside the palace."

"Then that should not be too difficult for you, my lord. You are Lorinthian Guard are you not?"

"We believe the king has defected."

"What?!" exclaimed the Vicar.

"All the Vicars are in danger. Umbra Lakar has ..."

"Who is it, lord Vicar?" said a resounding voice. Out stepped Marin from the distance.

"Ah, Captain Orilin," he said.

Orilin smiled.

"I was hoping to see you soon, Marin. It's good to know that you are alive!"

The two clasped arms.

"Marin," said Orilin. "We have to get into the palace. We believe the king has joined the Meldron sorceress."

Marin was shocked.

"Wha..."

"Marin," continued Orilin. "I know it is hard to believe but we have eyewitnesses, and if I am wrong you can do with me as you please. They have captive my wife. Besides, if all the Vicars have been summoned to the palace then there the sorceress awaits them, not to mention the king and the defected Guard."

Marin shook his head and sighed.

"You're asking me to lay siege to the palace, Captain."

There was a silence. Taelin then spoke up.

"It is true that the king has defected, my lord. Upon

my life it is true. I am page to his Majesty, and the sorceress …"

"How do you know this?" asked Marin gruffly.

"My lord," said Taelin. "I am page to his Majesty, and I was sent to Captain Orilin by the sorceress. She heard reports that he was still alive in Gallinthrar and lures him here to kill him. If not by her own blade then by the blade of the Guard."

"You speak bold for a boy," said Marin. "What is preventing me from nailing you to the ground this instant?"

"Truth, my lord. Truth."

Orilin stepped up.

"Marin, if Umbra Lakar is in the palace, everyone is in grave danger, especially the Vicars. There is no Flame to defend them. Listen, if things there are well, then we can just go in. If things are not, obviously, we will be attacked.

"Marin," continued Orilin. "The Guard have the right to enter the palace."

He then stepped in front of the rest of the gathered Guard.

"Men, if I am lying, then treat me as a traitor. But if not, then will you fight with me?"

They didn't know how to respond.

"Whether this story of defection is true or not we have a duty to Caltirion's people. I know we are the Queen's Guard and it is to the death for her Majesty. But if her Majesty has defected then we now have no queen to fight for. We have only the people of Caltirion and the Vicars."

Orilin sighed.

"This is not just about my wife," he said. "This is about defeating this sorceress. Either way, we must see to the palace's safety."

There was a long silence. Marin then stepped up.

"I will see to the palace's safety, Captain," he said. "If …"

"You have a duty to protect the Vicars as well, lord Marin," said Ulthrel. "All the more reason."

Marin nodded.

"All right," he said. "I will go."

The rest of the Guard slowly nodded and stepped up to Orilin.

"Let us go to attend to the palace's safety then," said Orilin.

He then looked to Taelin.

"You are a hero, Taelin," he said. "Go back to Commander Lardin and seek shelter.

ɤ ɤ ɤ ɤ ɤ ɤ

They went as a tight group. Orilin was in the lead. As they approached the front of the gates of the palace they noticed that many of the Guard were walking through the gates.

"Thank the Creator!" said Orilin. "Let us join them. We will gain entrance through the gates. But let us stay together."

The group of them joined about a hundred of the Guard. Orilin was sure to wear his helmet and put up his shield over the hawk's emblem on his breastplate. All of the Guard were marching like that with spears in hand. They were led through the gates and went through to the front gardens of the palace. As they stopped they snapped to attention. King Lyrinias came out from the inner courts to meet them in the gardens fully armed and armored. The wind swept over the battlements and there was a chill in the air.

"I have called you forth in terrible times," said Lyrinias. "With much reluctance it is by official decree of his and her Majesty that Orilin Alandiron must be hunted down in this city and put to death. He is guilty of high treason by threatening the life of the king and betrayal of the Guard."

Some of the Guard's eyes widened a bit.

"Furthermore," said Lyrinias. "Command of the Guard shall be personally overseen by me for the duration of this battle."

Orilin stepped out from among them and took off his helmet.

"The Guard will not be commanded by a traitor, Lyrinias!"

The Guard looked to each other. Lyrinias smiled.

"Brother. You have just signed your own death sentence."

Orilin looked to him.

"You think that these men believe that I would betray king and country after nearly one hundred years of service in the Guard?"

Lyrinias smiled again, but Orilin continued.

"You have allowed a Meldron sorceress to enter your chambers and take the Vicars hostage. And you have imprisoned and abused my wife. Where is she, Lyrinias?!" Lyrinias held up his hand.

"I …"

"Where is she?!" yelled Orilin.

Lyrinias grinned.

"Kill him."

Some of the Guard struck but Marin let loose his spear. He impaled the Guardsman trying to strike at Orilin.

"Men!" shouted Orilin. "Form ranks and strike!"

Orilin's men held up their shields and struck. The Guard waged war on themselves. Marin gathered up his spear and let it loose again. Orilin unsheathed the Malanthar and hewed his way towards the king. Lyrinias at the same time attacked the Guard fighting on Orilin's side. It was soon that all fighting for Orilin circled around him with their shields.

"Let me through!" yelled Orilin.

Marin let him pass.

Lyrinias and Orilin squared off.

"Brother!" yelled Orilin. "Come to your senses! You know what is right."

Swords clashed.

"You have allowed this Meldron sorceress to warp you."

Lyrinias laughed.

"The Divine Secret is mine, brother. Soon immortality will be mine, and you will be a dead man."

Swords met again. Lyrinias parried and held up his shield. Orilin's sword came crashing down on it and split it in two. Orilin then tossed his shield aside.

"I will defeat you honorably, brother, even if you are a traitor."

Lyrinias chuckled.

"You are quite foolish."

Swords met again.

"Please!" yelled Orilin. "I don't want to kill you, brother."

The fighting continued. Orilin parried. The Malanthar lit up with the Flame. It sliced through Lyrinias's sword. Lyrinias went for a spear and cast it at Orilin. He dodged it but it sliced him slightly on the cheek. He winced and held it a bit as the blood ran down.

"You are finished, dear brother," said Lyrinias. "You should have joined us."

He went for another spear, and he hefted it. Orilin attacked. Lyrinias tried in vain to block. Orilin sliced through the spear and through Lyrinias's midsection. The Flame erupted and Lyrinias's midsection was hewn open. The blood flew and the king dropped to his knees and then fell to the ground. Orilin winced and stood there for a moment. He then knelt there by the king holding him in his arms. All of a sudden the memories of them went through Orilin's mind. Their rides in the countryside. Their sparring. Their storytelling. All of the memories.

"How I loved you, brother," said Orilin with tears welling up in his eyes.

The king gasped, choking on his own blood as he was swiftly dying.

"Orilin," he said simply.

Then he slipped into death. Orilin slowly closed his eyes and shut the king's eyelids weeping as he did so.

Chapter 20

Ralharin drew his sword and attacked. Cyrus dodged and jumped towards the Flame with his staff. He dipped the tip of his staff in the Flame and the whole staff was illumined with its brightness. Sword and staff met.

"You were most foolish to fight me in this Temple, Ralharin. Here the Flame will consume you."

"And here you will die right where you received the Flame, Cyrus. Here it, mixed with your blood, will go out!"

Sword and staff met again. Cyrus smote Ralharin behind the knees and knocked him down. Ralharin flipped up and smashed Cyrus with a gust of wind. Cyrus flew through the air but dropped to his feet.

"My blood will not put out the Flame, Ralharin," he said. "And your sorcery will not put it out either."

Hhrin-Calin stepped up.

"Combined with mine it will, Cyrus," he said. He extended his staff toward Ralharin and received a bolt of lightning. His staff was charged with it and he flew it at Cyrus. Cyrus blocked it with his flamed staff. The combat went on and on. It was taking all of Cyrus's might to fend off both the traitor Arch-Vicar and the Meldron sorcerer. Cyrus blocked Ralharin's lightning but Hhrin-Calin saw an opening. He blasted Cyrus with a bolt and knocked him back against the wall. Cyrus dropped his staff and grabbed his head.

"Kill him," ordered Ralharin to Hhrin-Calin and the other two Meldron.

The Arch-Vicar stepped forward with lightning charging in his staff. Cyrus looked up helplessly not knowing what to do. Suddenly, there was a burst of the Flame from atop one of the pillars of the Temple. It blasted the Arch-Vicar back several feet. Two arrows shot out of the distance slaying the two Meldron sorcerers.

"Whoo hoo!" yelled Nalin.

The Wood Fay jumped down with the Flame lit in his right hand. Zarkaia came out with him armed with her bow.

"What?!" yelled Ralharin. "Who are you?!"

Nalin laughed.

"The Vicar of Niodath you fool!"

He threw the Flame at Ralharin, but he dodged. The Meldron looked upon the Fay with hatred.

"Then you will die here too, you little vexatious sprite!"

Nalin laughed and flipped and dodged the lightning. Zarkaia bent her bow and aimed it at Ralharin. She let loose her arrow but Hhrin-Calin deflected it with a gust of wind.

"This is not your fight, Zarkaia," he said. "Go back to your cloistered forests."

"Only to have them enveloped in your treachery and darkness, Hhrin-Calin? Or should I say, Calin?"

The Arch-Vicar blasted out lightning and blew her against the walls knocking her out. Cyrus then got up and readied his staff. It still glowed with the Flame.

"Hhrin-Calin!" he yelled. "Come back to reason! Come back to the light. There is no Divine Secret. In your path there is only death."

Hhrin-Calin looked to Cyrus and raised his hands. His eyes then glowed with fire.

"Cyrus, if the lightning with not take you then the fire will!"

He blasted a stream of fire at Cyrus who blocked it with the Flame. The flames blew fiercely among them.

"Hhrin-Calin!" yelled Cyrus. "Stop this madness. I give you one last chance."

Hhrin-Calin laughed.

"Stupid old Elf!" he said. "You yourself are clearly out of chance!"

Cyrus ran up to Hhrin-Calin while still blocking the fire and smote him in the jaw with his staff. He smote him again in the head.

"Your sorcery is no match for the Flame, Hhrin-Calin!"

The Arch-Vicar's eyes went wide. Cyrus smote him under the knees and knocked him down. He then dragged him across to the dais of the Flame.

"Hhrin-Calin, I hearby de-frock you as Arch-Vicar. Let the Flame deal with you as it wishes."

Cyrus then heaved him into the Flame and it consumed him.

"Aghh!" yelled the Arch-Vicar. He tried to gather the Flame into his hands but it was to no avail. He reached around desperately trying to control the Flame, but it was useless.

"Curse you, Cyrus!" he yelled. "Curse you!"

The flesh was then seared off his bones. Cyrus looked on as a skeleton started to replace flesh.

"Aghh!" he screamed again. The Arch-Vicar then turned to ash upon the dais.

ᛉ ᛉ ᛉ ᛉ ᛉ ᛉ

Orilin ran through the gates to the inner part of the palace. There he was met by two of the Guard.

"We cannot let you pass, Orilin," they said.

Orilin looked on in rage.

"Are you all duped?!"

They then attacked him. Orilin put up his shield as a sword came crashing down upon it. The other swept with his sword at his knees. Orilin blocked it and kicked his attacker in the jaw.

"Get away!" yelled Orilin. "I don't want to kill you!"

But the Guardsmen kept attacking. Orilin blocked with the Malanthar and parried. He then pushed one of the Guard with his shield, spun around and smashed his shield into the head of the other Guard.

"Do you leave me with no choice?" he yelled. "I am not a criminal!"

The two kept up their attack and Orilin continued to block. He slashed through the knee of one, and he fell to the ground. He then bashed his shield into the other. The one who fell picked up his sword and sliced through part of Orilin's thigh.

"Aghh!" he yelled in pain.

Orilin then spun around and slashed him through the throat. He faced the other Guardsman with his sword up on his shield; the blood running down his leg.

"You are crippled," said the Guardsman. "Don't make me kill you like this."

Orilin laughed a bit.

"So you want to hang me instead?"

The Guardsman attacked. Orilin bent down and impaled him with the Malanthar. The man screamed and looked up to Orilin with hatred.

"To …" he said. "To … death for her Majesty!"

Orilin shook his head.

"You have no Queen, friend. But you didn't know."

Orilin wrenched his sword free and hobbled away. He then fell to the ground in pain and sliced off a piece of one of his foe's tunics. Orilin then made a bandage out of it tying it tightly around his injured leg. It was enough to control the bleeding.

Next he made his way into the throne room. He grimaced in pain as he entered. What he saw terrified him. There lay, all over the ground, the Vicars. They were all slain with their throats sliced. Above them stood Umbra Lakar on the steps to the throne. With her was Queen Lirana. Orilin was enraged.

"Halt, Orilin!" said the queen. "Do …"

Umbra held up her hand.

"I will deal with him, you wench."

Lirana backed away a bit. Orilin approached the throne.

"You killed the Vicars?" he asked. Umbra smiled.

"Of course."

"And you have my wife?"

"Naturally," said Umbra.

"And I understand you kicked her and slapped her?"

Umbra laughed.

"She is such a baby, your wife. I'll kick and slap that dry vine all I want once I'm through with you!"

"You will not," said Orilin.

Umbra laughed again.

"You are stupid, Elf. You have no idea …"

But Orilin attacked. Umbra met him. The Flame erupted in the Malanthar and Orilin struck. He sliced Umbra through the midsection and she was flayed in half. Lirana stood stunned as the Meldron sorceress was killed instantly. She backed up in terror and looked at Orilin. Orilin wiped Umbra's blood off him and pointed the Malanthar to the queen.

"Lead me to Larilyn."

Lirana quickly obeyed.

It was now early in the evening. Lirana led Orilin down a flight of long stairs outside the throne room. Sconces lit the way and they came to a long hallway. Sconces lit that way as well. They both came to two Lorinthian Guard.

"Step aside," said the queen.

"My lady?!" they said. "This is a wanted man!"

"And I am Queen," she said. "I order you to step aside."

They bowed and did so. The largest of the men took out an iron key and unlocked the door. They came into a dank dungeon that smelled of mildew. There were two sconces on the wall that lit up the place, and Larilyn was chained to the wall.

"Orilin!" she gasped. Bruises were on her face, and she looked pale.

"Did the Guard do this to her, Lirana?" asked Orilin.

The queen did not answer. A Guard stepped up behind him.

"We did it, Elf," he sneered.

Orilin jumped out and spun around. He slashed and cleaved through the helmet of his first foe. The second Guardsman was caught totally unaware. He attacked Orilin with his spear. Orilin shattered it with the Malanthar, swept up with the sword and slashed through his throat and jaw. He then turned around and put his sword up to Lirana. He was starting to grow pale.

"You are losing blood, Orilin," said the queen. "Any minute the rest of the Guard will find you and kill you both."

"Why shouldn't I kill you?" gasped Orilin.

The queen raised her hands.

"Here I am. Your choice. Either you die of blood loss or the Guard finds my dead body here and puts you to death."

Orilin felt his strength failing. He dropped to his knees and dropped the Malanthar.

"Orilin!" cried Larilyn.

The queen smirked. She pushed Orilin over onto his back with her foot and grabbed the Malanthar. Orilin looked up and grabbed his leg. The pain was increasing. He had spent all of his strength fighting through Guard after Guard, the Meldron sorceress, his friend Lyrinias and now he didn't have the strength to defend himself or Larilyn. Lirana stood over him and sneered.

"So ends it. So ends the greatest warrior of Caltirion. And when the Great One comes, it will begin my immortality."

"No!" cried Larilyn.

Orilin looked on and gasped; the pain welling through his leg. He readied himself to receive the death blow. He looked to Larilyn and reached for her.

"I'm sorry, love," he said.

Lirana raised the Malanthar aloft, ready to deal Orilin his death blow. Suddenly the Flame erupted in the sword. Lirana felt her hands tingle at first. Then there was the burning.

"Aghh!" she screamed as she dropped the Malanthar like a hot iron. But her hands kept burning. Smoke rose from them as they slowly burned a charred black. Orilin looked on and groaned.

"You …," he gasped. "Should not … have touched the sword, Lirana."

The queen's body started to become a charred black.

"What … did you do to me, Elf?" she hissed.

Orilin winced with glazed eyes.

"It was you, Lirana," he said. "It was you … who … dabbled with them."

Smoke rose from her body and the hair fizzled out. Blue flame burst forth from her mouth and eyes. She screamed out and Orilin crawled over to cradle Larilyn.

"Aghhhh!" screamed Lirana.

The blue Flame erupted. The flesh quickly burnt from her body, and soon all that was left were parts of a skeleton left upon the ground; the blue Flame still coming from it. Orilin painfully crawled over to the sword and picked it up. It still glowed with the Flame. He sliced Larilyn's chains off the wall, dropped the sword and cradled his wife in his arms.

"It's over, love," he whispered. "It's over."

Larilyn looked into his eyes.

"No, love," she whispered. "I will get you help."

Orilin smiled.

"There is no help to get," he said.

He smiled at her. "All I … want to do now … at the end … is die in your arms."

Larilyn shook her head with tears streaming. She looked to his leg. The bandage was obsolete and his leg was soaked in blood.

"No, love," she cried. "I will … I will get you help."

She screamed.

"Someone help!"

Orilin collapsed on the floor. She laid herself on him.

"No!" she panicked. "Orilin!" Suddenly there was a commotion outside. Marin Kar and his few remaining men came down the stairs.

"Dame Larilyn!" he yelled.

"Yes!" she screamed. "Come help him!"

ᆺᆺᆺᆺᆺᆺ

Nalin was blown back by a huge wind. Ralharin then launched lightning out at Cyrus, who blocked it with the Flame. Zarkaia had hit her head and was still out. Cyrus tried to strike Ralharin with his staff but it was to no avail. Ralharin blocked it with his sword and kicked Cyrus upon the dais; his head hitting the pavement.

"Now you die, Cyrus. Now your blood will snuff out this idolatrous Flame. The Divine Secret will be revealed."

Cyrus looked up, holding his head.

"Do what you have to do, Ralharin," he said solemnly. "There is no Divine Secret. You will plunge Telbyrin into Chaos."

Ralharin laughed and raised his sword. Suddenly Nalin came from behind and kicked the Meldron in the back. Ralharin flew around and struck with his blade. Nalin dodged and flipped up to the dais to try to grab some of the Flame. Ralharin parried back. Nalin tossed a piece of the Flame to Cyrus who grabbed it and held it aloft.

"There, Cyrus!" yelled Nalin. "Finish him!"

Cyrus stood up and held the Flame above his head. Ralharin quickly attacked with a blow to the head but the Flame enveloped the blade and Ralharin was burned.

"Ahh!" he yelled backing up and dropping his blade.

He held his face between his hands. Cyrus then grabbed him by the shoulders.

"Just like ol' times, ah Ralharin!"

The Meldron looked on in hatred with his flesh starting to burn. Cyrus looked at him square in the eye.

"Let us go into the Flame itself! If I am to die then I am taking you with me!"

Cyrus flung him with all his might into the roaring Flame upon the dais. Ralharin grabbed him and both of them went in.

Ralharin saw blue all around. He heard it roaring. He heard the sound. The tiny sound that grew louder. It was almost like everything was singing. He saw the stars, the trees, the rivers. Everything in Telbyrin was seen in the Flame. Everything … sang.

"Do you hear it, Ralharin?" yelled Cyrus. "You cannot stop it!"

Ralharin screamed and tried to close his ears. But it was to no avail. The sound grew louder. Cyrus stood enveloped in the Flame with arms raised aloft singing a song of praise to the Creator in the old Elven speech of Laerdiron. Ralharin sank and closed his ears again.

"You cannot stop it!" shouted Cyrus. "And this is your final apostasy, Ralharin. You will die with the Song in your ears!"

Ralharin screamed. The Song was unbearable. He tried in vain to seek the darkness, but it was not granted him. All he saw was the light and the sound … oh the sound … oh the awful sound of the Song. He screamed again as he was being burned. Not only his body, but his mind.

"Cyrus!" he yelled. "Stop this sound!"

Cyrus looked down on him.

"I cannot stop it. All creation sings it. You will die in the very thing you have hated; the light."

Ralharin roared in anger and reached, trying to get out. But it was to no avail. It was not so much the Flame that hurt but the sound of the Song. Ralharin screamed one last time as the Flame erupted around him, consuming him. He was incinerated into a shadow which simply passed out of the Flame.

Barras-Drin and some of his men then entered the Temple. When they entered they saw the Flame roaring all the way to the summit. It was as big and as bright as they had ever seen it. Inside it stood Cyrus holding his arms aloft and his eyes blazing with the Flame. Every bit of his being was enveloped in the Flame. He was one with the Eternal Song and one with the Flame.

"Leave Barras-Drin!" he said. "Leave and return here no more!" The outlaw stumbled back and ran from the Temple along with his men.

Chapter 21

They took Orilin to the physician's room atop the palace. They laid him atop a couch. Enoa was waiting for them.

"He is dying," said Larilyn.

Enoa sighed, feeling his pulse.

"His pulse is still strong, dear," she said.

She then looked at the gash on Orilin's leg.

"Give him water, Marin," she said. Marin obeyed.

Orilin drank from the waterskin, slipping in and out of consciousness. Larilyn looked on, holding both his hands.

"Orilin," she whispered in his ear. "Please do not Fade. Please. You have a reason to live. See," she said placing his hand on her stomach.

"I can feel him, Orilin," she said. "I know he is there. I know. I just know. Our shame is over."

Enoa smiled, knowing that Larilyn was right.

"Orilin," said Larilyn. "We can still have our dream." She started to weep.

"We can still have our dream on the farm. We can still have our little one. We can still have everything we dreamed of. A life without war. A life without violence. Just me, you and our little one with the cows. The little river past the Kesstals' farm. Strolls through the Forest of Beth. The stars at night. I still want to share it all with you, Orilin."

He groaned a little and looked up at her.

"Larilyn."

She squeezed his hands.

"Yes, love. Yes."

He was conscious again.

"We … can have our dream."

She wiped some more tears away.

"Yes, love. Yes we can."

Enoa irrigated the wound and then dressed it with coagulate. She then put a fresh dressing on it.

Orilin then slipped out of consciousness.

"The fever is growing," said Enoa. "Get me a cool rag."

Marin obeyed and they put the rag atop Orilin's head.

"I don't know if he will make it, Dame Larilyn," said Enoa.

Larilyn looked to her.

"He has a reason to go on," she said meekly.

Enoa looked to her.

"Do you want to be with him?"

Larilyn nodded.

"If … if he is to pass … then I want to be with him."

Enoa nodded.

"Everyone out except myself and Dame Larilyn."

Everyone obeyed. Enoa sat over him, and Larilyn continued to caress his hands.

"Please, love," she said. "Don't Fade on me."

Orilin then took a deep breath. Larilyn was wide-eyed. Enoa felt of his neck.

"I will give him some ether to help him sleep and then stitch up his wound."

Larilyn looked to her and nodded.

Enoa went to work stitching up the wound. After the ether, Orilin slept soundly. Larilyn never left his side. There was then a gentle knock at the door.

"Come in," said Enoa.

Marin entered.

"The Meldron have retreated. Caltirion's cavalry re-mustered, and with Gallinthrar's help, we have routed them. There are heavy losses though."

Enoa closed her eyes, and Larilyn looked to Marin.

"It is over then?"

Marin nodded.

"I will leave you to him now."

He closed the door gently behind him.

"Dame Larilyn," said Enoa. "I have done all I can do for your husband. I have to report with the rest of the physicians to save what number we can."

Larilyn nodded.

"I understand," she whispered. "I won't leave him."

$$\Upsilon\,\Upsilon\,\Upsilon\,\Upsilon\,\Upsilon\,\Upsilon$$

Orilin slept for another whole day. Larilyn looked out her window to the west. There was a glittering light in the distance. It grew and grew. Suddenly Larilyn recognized it as the Airell Elven host. She closed her eyes and sighed. At least they were here to help re-build Caltirion. She knew Elrad would be among them. She would have to take him to Orilin. She looked back at him. He was still asleep, but his breathing was steady. She went and gently laid herself atop his breast. She could feel his heartbeat. It was slow but steady.

"Orilin," she sighed. She lay there for moments more. His heartbeat picked up speed a bit and his breathing deepened. She looked down at him. A couple of tears hit his cheeks.

"Come back to me," she said.

Elrad led the Elven host into the city. It was in shambles. The Elves started to help tend the wounded. They were a welcome sight. Hadar and Marin met up with Elrad.

"Just in time, eh?" Hadar said jokingly. Elrad grinned.

"It's a long journey from the Airells, but we were willing. I'm glad we can help re-build."

He looked around.

"Whatever happened to the Meldron sorceress?"

"She is dead," said Marin. "Orilin slew her."

Elrad smiled and nodded.

"I knew he would not fail. I can only hope things are well in Al-Nartha."

Hadar looked at Elrad's staff where the Flame burned brightly.

"It seems so, lord Vicar."

Elrad looked at the Flame and smiled.

"Where is Orilin?"

Marin's face went serious.

"He is injured. Dame Larilyn is with him."

Elrad's face turned downcast.

"Take me to him."

Marin and Hadar led Elrad up the palace battlements. People were tending to the wounded and to the dead.

"Lord Vicar," said Hadar. "The Vicars of Caltirion have been slain. They are preparing them for burial in the Sanctuary gardens."

Elrad turned around in grief.

"And the acolytes?"

"They have escaped. Young Shamil is among them."

Elrad nodded.

"I will need to see him. Captain, I dreaded this. But for now, take me to Orilin."

Elrad made his way up to the physician's room. He knocked gently.

"Come in," said a female voice. Elrad entered and found Larilyn holding Orilin.

"I'm so glad you're here," she said.

Elrad sighed deeply, came over and touched Orilin's

hand.

"My son."

Larylin looked up to him.

"I don't know what to do," she said.

"There is not much you can do, Dame Larilyn."

"He has a reason to live," she cried. Elrad looked away to the outside.

"What reason is that?"

Larilyn looked to him.

"I am with child."

Elrad's eyes widened. He walked over to Orilin.

"My son," he whispered. "Awaken. You most certainly have a reason to live. Awaken, my son."

Orilin breathed deeply again. Larilyn looked to Elrad.

"Is there anything else we can do?"

Elrad looked to her.

"There remains only one option, but, of course, it could be fatal."

"The Flame?" asked Larilyn.

Elrad nodded.

"It will not kill him," she said. "It didn't kill him in Gallinthrar, and I don't believe it will kill him now."

"There is always a chance," said Elrad.

Larilyn shook her head.

"I don't believe it."

She looked down to Orilin.

"Love," she said. "I want to use the Flame on you to heal you."

Orilin squeezed her hand a bit.

"He is gaining consciousness," said Larilyn.

Elrad knelt beside him.

"Very well, my son. Relax. You are a hero of Telbyrin. Relax, now."

Elrad placed the Flame in Orilin's wound.

Orilin groaned a bit.

Larilyn looked to him and squeezed his hands tight. The Flame burned brightly in the wound and started to seal it up. As it sealed, Orilin's breathing grew more relaxed. When the wound was healed, Elrad removed the Flame. Larilyn looked to Orilin. His eyes were still closed.

"Love," she said.

He squeezed her hands.

"I … I always wanted some cream-colored cows," he said.

Larilyn's eyes grew bright.

"Orilin!"

He gently opened his eyes and looked at her.

"The red ones are so overrated."

Larilyn laughed and embraced him. He smiled and kissed her. She laughed again.

"I could not leave you, farm girl," said Orilin. "I have so many reasons to live."

She pressed his hand to her stomach again.

"We … we will have to start thinking about names," she said.

He smiled and the two embraced again. Elrad stood there above them.

"May you and Larilyn be blessed, my son."

Orilin looked up to him.

"Thank you, father."

ᕕᕗᕕᕗᕕᕗ

Days passed as the citizens of Caltirion went about the task of rebuilding. The morale of the city slowly crept back into it. Elrad tended to the people as well as Ulthrel, Lau and Shamil. The Airell Elves stood on for days, helping. Guards were stationed up on the battlements again. Commander Lardin took control over his remaining men and gave them command to look after their families. Hadar, Torla, as well as the men of Gallinthrar, returned to their city.

It was at the end of one day, in the early evening as the sun was making its way toward the west that the guards spotted a lone figure riding toward the south city gates. The gates were opened and the traveler was allowed in. It was Raltaron. People, especially the Airell Elves rejoiced to see him. Elrad ran up.

"Vicar Raltaron!" he said. "What news from the south? What news from Al-Nartha?" Raltaron dismounted and came up to them all. Orilin and Larilyn emerged from the crowd.

"The Flame has been restored and burns brightly at Al-Nartha and the Sanctuaries."

"What happened?" asked Elrad. "What caused it all?" Raltaron smiled.

"An old acquaintance and I met up again – one who did not want to join in the Song. But he faded like a shadow. It is over. It is all over."

"Who was it?" asked Elrad.

Raltaron looked mildly irritated.

"Oh, Elrad," he said. "Must you ask so many questions? The Meldron prophecy was fulfilled."

"The Dark Resurgence?" asked Elrad. "Ralharin was resurrected?"

"For a time," said Raltaron. "But he is no more. Hhrin-Calin betrayed us all. He sought this Divine Secret for himself and no doubt aided in Ralharin's resurgence. But he is no more. Let us go to the Sanctuary."

They all followed Raltaron there, and many were assembled. The remaining Vicars gathered around Raltaron. Elrad spoke up.

"With no Arch-Vicar, who will install the next? Who will lead us?"

Raltaron smiled.

"That would be you, dear Elrad. Do you accept?"

Elrad was speechless.

"Raltaron. You are …"

"I am more than I seem, Elrad. I already have had you much in mind for this task. It took all my strength to defeat Ralharin. This is my last task as your Patriarch – indeed, my last task for Telbyrin. Please kneel."

Elrad looked up to him.

"Lord Cyrus?!"

Raltaron nodded.

"I have lain hidden for thousands of years under the name Raltaron, making sure that the Dark Resurgence would never be fulfilled. But never did I suspect that one of our own number would aid in such a thing. Ralharin made an ever-lasting threat to our world, and I could not Fade until I made sure that the threat was quelled. I cannot delay, Elrad. My time is upon me, and the Creator is calling me unto the halls of the blessed. Please kneel."

Elrad did so.

"Elrad, I charge you to guard the Flame of Telbyrin with all devotion and reverence. I charge you to ordain Vicars to protect the lands and the races, making known to them all of their Supreme Protector, the Creator. The Unnamable One. I install you as Arch-Vicar of Telbyrin to make known and to sound forth the joining of the Eternal Song. May the Creator be praised forever."

"May the Creator be praised forever" replied Elrad.

Cyrus then lay his hands on Elrad's head for a few moments then bid him rise.

"Rise, Hhrin-Elrad!"

The people roared in applause. Elrad was handed Cyrus's staff and looked over to Orilin and Larilyn, who came up to him.

"Father?" said Orilin.

"Pray for me, my son."

Orilin nodded slowly and looked over to Cyrus. He bowed.

"My Patriarch."

Cyrus grinned and bid him rise.

"I told you, young one, that more would be revealed to you in time. You have listened, and in your listening you have saved many. My thanks to you."

Cyrus then walked over to Larilyn. She bowed and then looked up to him. Cyrus smiled.

"You're not such a common farm-punch after all, young lass."

She laughed a bit.

"No, Patriarch."

Cyrus lay his hand on her right shoulder.

"The blessing of the Creator be upon you, Larilyn. May your embarrassments be gone and may you and your husband be always blessed."

Cyrus then walked over to Elrad and blessed all the people. All the Elves bowed. Cyrus then sat down on one of the steps of the Sanctuary.

"Hhrin-Elrad," he said. "I am feeling unusually weak."

"No, Patriarch," said Elrad. "You cannot Fade on us now. Please."

Cyrus looked up to him and chuckled.

"All things Fade, Hhrin-Elrad. All but the Creator and the Eternal Song. Let an old Elf go to his reward. I will always look down on you. Always. There is nothing to fear. Lead them."

Elrad took his hands in his. Grey ash was coming off of them.

"Lord Patriarch," said Elrad.

"I can see it," said Cyrus. "Oh, how beautiful it is. How beautiful."

His body began to turn grey. It grew and grew in color. Cyrus closed his eyes. A gentle wind came and gently swept the ashes away.

Chapter 22

Months passed. Caltirion was re-furbished. It and Gallinthrar saw to the peace and re-establishment of Sargna. Hhrin-Elrad ordained more Vicars in the place of the slain ones. Shamil was among them. Commander Lardin was awarded the Shield of Valor. It was the highest military honor of Caltirion. After the mourning for the Fading of Cyrus, the Airell Elves made their way back to the Enclave. All but two. Iomil and Oandor looked around desperately trying to find Orilin and Larilyn.

"Where are Dame Larilyn and Captain Orilin, Commander?" she asked Commander Lardin.

"They are leaving, my lady."

"For where?"

Lardin smiled.

"Back to Sargna. There they want to start their lives afresh. Orilin gave the Malanthar to Marin Kar."

Iomil smiled a bit.

"I must find her. I am still her maidservant."

Iomil and Oandor found them among some traders making their way to Gallinthrar.

"Mistress!" Iomil cried out. "Dame Larilyn!"

Larilyn looked back.

"Iomil?!"

The two embraced and smiled.

"I and Oandor won't leave you, mistress," she said.

Larilyn laughed a bit.

"I suppose we could use some more hands on the farm."

She looked to Orilin who smiled and nodded.

"There you have it!" said Larilyn. "Iomil, are you sure you do not want to go to the Enclave?
It's …"

"How could I forsake my lady?" she said. "And how could I forsake my friend?"

Larilyn smiled.

"My friend," she said. "I like that better."

Iomil smiled and took Oandor's hand.

"I have been released from military service, Captain Orilin," he said.

Orilin grinned at him.

"Just 'Orilin' from this point, my friend."

Oandor smiled back and they clasped each other's arms.

The journey back to Sargna was relatively peaceful. They started to notice the little farms here and there; the windmills and the gardens. They crossed over into Acaida and stayed the night.

The night was a crisp cool one with bright stars. Ethlaharin and Hilmod shown bright. Orilin was seeing to their horses when a familiar voice rang out in the distance.

"All is well. All is well," he said.

A little old woman followed the Vicar.

"Vicar Elimed," she said. "We are so thankful to …"

"Thank the Creator," said Elimed. "And may you be blessed."

He walked on a little farther.

"Now," he said. "Where is that farrier?"

"Elimed!" shouted Orilin. The Vicar looked over in his direction.

"Ah, Orilin?! Thank the Creator. Orilin!"

The two Elves met in an embrace.

"So, uh," Elimed stuttered. "How was your time in Caltirion?"

Orilin laughed.

"We have much to talk about. Where are the Kesstals?"

Elimed smiled.

"Follow me, lad. Follow me!"

Elimed led the rest of the Elves into a cozy tavern. It was a very respectable establishment. The Kesstals were about to have dinner. Alanna looked up.

"Orilin!" she screamed. "Larilyn!" She ran over to Larilyn, and the Elf bent down and embraced her.

"My little sister!" she said. "How are you?" Alanna laughed and noticed Larilyn's belly.

"Larilyn!" she said. "You're having … you're having a …"

"Yes," said Larilyn. "We believe it's going to be a boy. But this is just the first. We want to have more. A girl, too." Alanna laughed.

Alander, Zitha and Drelas joined them in embraces. Elimed pulled up another table and joined the two. The families sat down to a rather large dinner. Drelas and Alanna told the Elves about all their adventures with the Wood Fays of the Niodath Forests. They said that Vicar Nalin and Zarkaia made their way back from Al-Nartha and let them go. There was some sad news as well. The Kesstals had lost their farm to the Menetarrans. Trealin and his family eventually made their way to the Niodath forests and were later set free. They were trying to establish a homestead in the Forest of Beth. The Kesstals had taken up temporary residence in Acaida and were planning what to do next. The kids said they wanted to move close to Trealin and his family, and that was certainly discussed.

"Are you going back into the cattle business?" asked Orilin.

Alander smiled.

"It's the only thing I know!   Going to have to get some somewhere. Don't know how I'm going to do it, though."

Elimed looked on.

"We will think of something!"

Days passed by, and Elimed sold many lavish furnishings out of his Vicarage. His excuse was that he didn't need all of it because it detracted from a Vicar's humility. Orilin and Larilyn knew something else was up.

The families were coaxed into settling within the Forest of Beth which was vast enough to welcome more homesteaders. The families found Trealin's family a couple of miles away through the forest. Funds mysteriously appeared for the Kesstals from an anonymous source. Orilin and Larilyn knew where and whence they came, but they did not say anything.

Orilin and Larilyn built their homestead gently within the forest beside a crystal clear lake which was small but very beautiful. Iomil and Oandor's homestead was not far away. A stream fed the lake beside Orilin and Larilyn's home to the left and a grove of cypress was around the house. Orilin and Larilyn would sit out on their deck during the evening and night and watch the birds, the sunset and the stars. All the while Larilyn's belly swelled more.

"I think I'm going in for the night," said Orilin late one evening.

Larilyn smiled.

"I will come shortly, love." Orilin smiled, kissed her and kissed her belly. She smiled, got up and went down by the lake. She silently said a prayer of thanksgiving to the Creator for all that was given to them.

"Small one," she said cradling her belly. "You have such a great father."

ᘺᘺᘺᘺᘺᘺ

The next day it was time to go to work. Orilin grabbed his tools and took Larilyn with him. She was going to just be

with them as she could not do much work. Alander and Zitha
met them.

"Ready?" asked Alander.

"Always," replied Orilin. "Let's rebuild your farm."
There was bawling in the distance and a lone figure was coming up to them. Orilin and Alander gazed at the figure and
smiled. It was Elimed. He met them on a large grassy hill.

"Well," he said. "I couldn't stand it. I had to help
re-build this farm. So I went to my first cattle auction. I was
quite unskilled at such a thing but my friend Arban the farrier
helped me quite a bit."

"Elimed?" asked Orilin. "What have you been up to?"

Elimed grinned.

"Come and see."

Elimed, Orilin and Alander made their way up the hill
and looked down. To Orilin's delight, there lay at the bottom
of the hill a herd of large, hungry cream-colored cows.

The End

People, Places,
Landmarks of Telbyrin

Acaida — Sargna's capital city.

Airell Mountains — The upper western mountain range of Telbyrin. The North Enclave of Elves is built there.

Alander Kesstal — A cattle farmer in West Sargna who hires Orilin.

Alanna Kesstal — Alander and Zitha Kesstal's daughter.

Aldanar — The Captain of the Lorinthian Guard when the story takes place.

Al-Nartha — Known as the Sacred City. In the ancient Elven speech, it means "The Spark." It is believed to be the center of the world; where the Creator first touched Telbyrin into existence. The main Flame is housed in a great Temple there. It is the Arch-Vicar's main residence.

Alriad — A great Elven king of Laerdiron. He used the Malanthar to help defeat the Meldron in the Battle of Rak-Mardan.

Alrihon the Great — The first king of Caltirion in recorded history.

Arch-Vicar — The successor of Cyrus; the chief of the ten original Vicars of Telbyrin. They can be from any race, although the Wood Fays have never accepted the position due to their seclusion in the Niodath Forests.

Armid — The North Elven Enclave's overseer.

Ash-Vargal — A battle between the forces of Caltirion, rebellious Hallintorian lords and the Meldron three years before the story begins. All rebellious lords against Caltirion were put down after this battle.

Barisath — The last queen of Laerdiron.

Barras-Drin — A dreaded outlaw from northeast Hallintor. He also has his own horde.

Bodar — The Captain of Cedar Grove's security forces.

Caltirion — The former capital of the empire of Hallintor. After the break-up of the empire due to rebellious lords, Hallintor was reduced to city-states. Caltirion remained the largest, most influential one.

Cedar Grove — A small hamlet outside of Gallinthrar.

Creator — Telbyrin's deity.

Cyrus — The Patriarch of all Elves and all Vicars. He was also chief of the original first ten Vicars of Telbyrin. He did not migrate with Alriad and the Elves who left Al-Nartha. He spent much of his life making sure that the Dark Resurgence would never take place. No one knows when or if he Faded.

Dark Resurgence — Dark Meldron prophecies foretelling the Meldron Patriarch Ralharin's resurrection.

Divine Secret — Known also as the Eternal Secret, it is the Meldron's doctrine of the hidden secrets of the Creator. They believe that it contains the secret of unity with the Creator and immortality. It is the direct opposite of the doctrine of the Eternal Song.

Dreath Wood — A haunted wood south of Gallinthrar. In it was the hamlet of Janlar where an uprising was started by a rebel named Kharlia.

Drelas Kesstal — Alander and Zitha Kesstal's son.

Elimed — Acaida's chief Vicar. He is a short, chubby

Elf.

Elrad — Orilin's father by adoption. He is one of Caltirion's most renown Elven Vicars.

Elves — The first race of Telbyrin who were entrusted with the Eternal Flame. Elves come in many shapes and sizes. They can be tall or short, robust or chubby, fair skinned or dark skinned. All have pointed ears. What unites them is that they are the race most in tune with the Eternal Song. The first ten Vicars of Telbyrin were all Elves under the Patriarchate of Cyrus. It was theorized that Cyrus was even the first Elf to awaken into existence. Nevertheless, all Elves hold him as their Patriarch. Elves usually live for a very long time growing more in tune with the Song throughout their lives. They must control the Passions that go against the Song, (gross hedonism, greed, lust, anger, etc.). If the Passions get too out of control, they Fade.

During the primordial age, many Elves migrated from Al-Nartha to the plains of Laerdiron. There the great city of Laerdiron was constructed which fell to the Meldron around 300 years before this story begins.

Enclave — A large Elven city. Elves have been trying to form them after the destruction of Laerdiron, their main city. There are two main Enclaves in Telbyrin: one in the Airell Mountains and one beneath Mt. Talindrir.

Enoa — A renowned physician of Caltirion.

Eternal Flame — The Sacred Flame revered by all the peoples of Telbyrin. It was what was left by the Creator touching Telbyrin into existence and symbolizes all of Telbyrin's prayers going up to the Creator. Only the Vicars of the Flame can handle it physically and use it to defend others.

Eternal Song — The praise that all the universe gives the Creator. It is believed, especially by the Elves, that all creation sings. The Song is eternal as the Creator is eternal. It holds much on the teachings on the afterlife in Telbyrin.

Ethlaharin — The star of Laerdiron. It is believed to be a guidepost to the great Elven city. It is the favorite star of the Elves because of the belief that it led many of them from Al -Nartha to the region of Laerdiron.

Fading — A process that Elves go through at the end of their lives. Out of all the races of Telbyrin, the Elves are most in tune with the Eternal Song. Their whole lives must maintain an equilibrium with the Song. Anything such as extreme anger, carnality, hedonism, sadness, or bloodlust fall into what the Elves call the Passions and, if not kept in check, can make them Fade. When an Elf sees that he or she is slipping grossly into the Passions, they can go on Quest, a process to reunite themselves to the Eternal Song. Elves can use humor, romance, beauty, art, music, and many other means to better unite themselves to the Song. But when they totally lose connection, they Fade. They can also Fade by being perfectly united to the Song in such a way that no higher praise can be given to the Creator in Telbyrin.

Forest of Beth — A beautiful forest in Sargna. Many small homesteads are there.

Gallinthrar —The city-state in Hallintor that is south of Caltirion.

Gila — Commander of Caltirion's forces.

Hadar — A Captain in Gallinthrar's forces.

Hadix — The Commander of Gallinthrar's forces.

Hallintor — The northern lands of Telbyrin. It is mainly of Human dwelling.

Hhrin — A word from the primordial language of Telbyrin meaning "great lord." It is the title of all the Arch-Vicars of Telbyrin.

Hhrin-Calin — The Human Arch-Vicar when the story takes place.

Hilmod — The star of Caltirion. It was said to have shown bright on Alrihon's birth and has remained Telbyrin's north star.

Hithena — Armid's wife.

Humans — The most numerous people of Telbyrin. Humans are diverse in culture; some largely nomadic (such as the Menetarrans), some living in large city-states (such as the Hallintorians) and some as simple homesteaders, farmers and town dwellers (such as the Sargnans). Humans have a large population of Vicars like the Elves and the two races largely are very friendly with each other.

Iomil — An Elven physician and handmaid to Dame Larilyn Alandiron.

Janlar — A hamlet in the Dreath Wood that caused an uprising against the lords of Gallinthrar. The hamlet and all associated with it were destroyed in the Battle of Janlar.

Karvol — The Meldron general who led the Hallintorian rebel lords against Caltirion. He was defeated in the Battle of Ash-Vargal.

Kharlia — The ghoulish spirit of the main rebel at Janlar who haunts the Dreath Wood. She was blinded for her rebellion.

Krinmarel — A large Menetarran city.

Laerdiron — The ancient Elven city to the North. It was destroyed by the Meldron the same year as the births of Orilin and Larilyn. Since then the Elves have largely been a scattered race throughout Telbyrin. The Plains of Laerdiron are named after it. Many Elves still dwell on those plains.

Lake Talaedrin — The largest body of water in Telbyrin. The river that feeds it flows from Al-Nartha. It lies in Menetarra.

Lardin — The Commander of Caltirion's infantry.

Larilyn Alandiron — Orilin Alandiron's wife. Before her marriage to Orilin, she was known as Larilyn Norin. She was orphaned as a babe after the destruction of Laerdiron and adopted by a Human couple named Bartlin and Treana Norin who lived in Sargna. After a long life of Quests, traveling and farm work, she hired on at Alander Kesstal's cattle farm. It was there that she fell in love with Orilin. Her first name simply means "dove."

Lau — Gallinthrar's chief Vicar.

Lirana — King Lyrinias's queen.

Lorinthia — Alrihon the Great's queen. She is the most revered and loved of all the queens of Caltirion's history.

Lorinthian Guard — Caltirion's most prized fighting force. Only the best most promising warriors can try out for a place in it. Known as the "Queen's Guard," it was named in honor of Alrihon the Great's queen, Queen Lorinthia. The Guard charges first in all battles and guards the Vicars and the royalty of Caltirion.

Lyrinias — Caltirion's Human king during the story. He was a very good friend of Orilin and the two considered themselves brothers.

Malanthar — The most powerful weapon in Telbyrin. It is a sword that was forged in the main Flame by Cyrus. The flame acts on its own inside the blade. The weapon cannot be broken. It is also known as the King's Sword and was given first to the Elven king of Laerdiron, Alriad, by Cyrus. Cyrus intended it to be a weapon to benefit all the people of Telbyrin so Alriad shared it with the Humans. It has remained in their possession since the destruction of Laerdiron.

Marin Kar — A young Human warrior in the Lorinthian Guard who shows great promise and leadership. He is deadly with the spear.

Martralin — Orilin Alandiron's former teacher in swordsmanship and war.

Meldron — Known as the Shadow People, this race dwells in darkness in the Mountains of Black seeking what is known as the Divine Secret. They did not accept the Flame in primordial days as they do not believe that they need it to give praise to the Creator or know the Creator. Ralharin, their Patriarch, cursed the Elves as idolaters. They are the arch-enemy of the Elves.

Menetarra — A Human region south and east of the Niodath Forests. The Humans there are largely nomadic except for the great cities of Krinmarel and Ulmilkar.

Mountains of Black — The north mountain region where the Meldron dwell in darkness.

Mountains of Rhdril — A mountain range south of the Plains of Lueldrin.

Mount Talindrir — The largest and tallest mountain in Telbyrin.

Nalin — The Wood Fay Vicar of the Niodath Forests.

Nesdarath — The dreaded black Meldron horses raised in the darkness of the Mountains of Black. They fear nothing and each know only one master.

Nidor — Commander of Caltirion's cavalry.

Niodath Forests — There are many forests and woods in Telbyrin but this is the largest and most ancient. The Wood Fays dwell there, a faerie race who generally does not deal with visitors kindly. They protect their forests very well. People can get lost in these forests and not come back out for some time.

Orilin Alandiron — One of the most renowned Elven warriors in Telbyrin. His first name means "Little Hawk." He was orphaned after the destruction of Laerdiron and was adopted by Vicar Elrad in Caltirion but left there periodically early in his life to go adventuring. He is also a very talented musician. After many Quests and much adventuring, he settled back in Caltirion and joined the ranks of the Lorinthian Guard at age 205. His best friend during his later life in Caltirion was Lyrinias. At age 298, he was honorably discharged from the Guard and settled in west Sargna on Alander Kesstal's farm. There he met Larilyn Norin and knew that he had found his soulmate at last.

Orinda Hallison — A seductive minstrel from Hallintor. She got her start in Caltirion.

Pilgrimage — The annual journey to Al-Nartha by the people of Telbyrin to venerate the Flame. Usually it is seasonal according to the region. Many people are content to make Pilgrimage to a local Sanctuary near them. Al-Nartha receives Pilgrims every day.

Plains of Lueldrin — A largely multicultural area where both Humans and Elves dwell. Much produce and live-stock go up to Al-Nartha from there.

Quest — A journey that an Elf can go on in order to better reunite with the Eternal Song. Sometimes they last for years. Going on Quest consist of much traveling around Telbyrin, taking in beauty and discovering new things about one's self. Another main purpose of them is to restrain the Passions.

Rak-Mardan — A great battle between the Elves of Laerdiron and the Meldron. Alriad and the Vicars led the Elves to victory over the Meldron who did not emerge out of the Mountains of Black for over a thousand years.

Ralharin — The Patriarch of the Meldron. He founded the doctrine of the Divine Secret and engaged in an epic battle with Cyrus in which he was defeated. No one knows when he died. The Meldron have tried to force his return through the Dark-Resurgence.

Raltaron — A powerful Vicar from the Airell Mountains.

Sargna — The northwest region of Telbyrin. It is mostly composed of farmers and cattle ranchers.

Taelin — A young Page to King Lyrinias.

Telbyrin — The world.

Telbyrin Wastes — A southern region in Telbyrin largely uninhabited. It is a place where many hermits and penitents dwell. It is rumored that even monsters dwell there.

Torla — Hadar's assistant.

Trealin — A homesteader that lives near the Kesstal farm. He watches the Kesstal family's cattle while they are away on Pilgrimage.

Ulmilkar — A large city in Menetarra.

Ulthrel — One of the chief Vicars in Caltirion. He serves as the guardian of the Sanctuary there.

Umbra Lakar — a dreaded Meldron sorceress. She is extremely powerful and has longed to aid the Meldron in the Dark Resurgence.

Vicars — The guardians of the Flame of Telbyrin. They only have the ability through the grace of their ordination to handle the Flame. They also serve the armies in Telbyrin using the Flame to help quell sorcery. One must serve as an acolyte for a long time in order to receive ordination. Then, after ordination, one places their hands into the Flame. All Vicars carry a staff in which the Flame can rest atop. Vicars wear white and gold robes. Vicars serve all the people of Telbyrin and are forbidden to take strict political sides in regional squabbles.

Wood Fays — The faerie race that dwells within the Niodath Forests. They are mostly cloistered within the Forests except when a few of them go on Pilgrimage. There are many legends and rumors about them. Some are true and some are not.

Zitha Kesstal — Wife of Alander Kesstal and mother to Drelas and Alanna Kesstal.

About the Author

Br. Benedict Dyar, O.S.B. is a solemnly professed Benedictine monk of St. Bernard Abbey in Cullman, AL. He was raised in Opelika, Alabama, and is a graduate of Athens State University, Athens, Alabama, with a degree in history. His love for fantasy adventure was first kindled in him as a young boy by the reading of J.R.R. Tolkien. Other than writing on the world of Telbyrin, Br. Benedict enjoys baking bread, music, and astronomy.

Made in the USA
Columbia, SC
18 July 2019